Tumblers

Also by the Author
The Hermit Ledger
Longitudes

contact the author seanblack40@gmail.com
Artwork by Albert Diezhandino
contact the artist at Albert@VioletandBlues.com

Copyright © 2011 Sean Black
All rights reserved.

ISBN: 1-4664-6265-5
ISBN-13: 9781466462656

Tumblers

Sean Black

Contents

My Smithsonian	1
In Fifths and Packs	11
More James Dean	29
Spiked Bats and Leather Boots	37
Half-Mast at Fort Knox	47
The Dharma Arsonist	53
Bravissimo	61
Vintage Chevy	69
Origins of August	85
The Downfall of Houli's	89
Racine	105
Better Than Disney	111
Revival of August	123
Chivalry's Not Dead	127
Faith in Electricity	141
The Ultimate Backfire	149
Her Good Friend Bad Luck	159

My Smithsonian

"I want you to do me on the living-room rug," Darla says. "It's *really* old. Like, knights-and-King-Arthur-shit old."

She is stumbling as she leads me through a maze of oak doorways. She's rambling, slurring her thoughts as fast as they come to her mind. Combined with a near-trip into a vase, it makes her look and sound adorably silly.

"All right, milady," I say, stumbling a little myself and chuckling under my breath, "wherever sounds fine." It's true; I do not mind. Guilt for a rug is not a luxury I am able to focus on; my rum-dulled conscience is strictly short-term.

We walk through a small chamber with an old Greek-looking statue in it. The wood walls are dark and polished, and the hardwood beneath the plush area rug is pristine. Darla is rich, but she likes to fuck me anyway. She likes to pretend she lives on the fringe; I'd fallen off the edge long ago. I guess that gives her something to admire in me, while giving me something to grab onto in her. She lives with her parents in this ancient house that smells of perfume and wood oil. I'm sure all of the furniture, the wall paintings, and the statues are antiques, but none of this makes the place feel whole, like a home. Instead, it just feels like a museum to me.

"How many other people have fucked on that rug before my family bought it?" she continues, using an arm along the wall to steady herself. "I want a memory on it besides opening Christmas presents or Dad kicking the dog for pissing on it."

2

"Of course, princess!" I say, holding a finger up to prove my point, nearly falling over backward. Darla is on a crusade to defile a rug, and I'm happy to play Lancelot to her Guinevere.

When we are done, I just lie there. It's been a long week; I'm back with quartermaster for the summer, moving military people in and out of their homes. It takes a lot out of you, all of that up and down stairs with boxes and couches. The local nationals, or "LNs" as they are popularly known through military anachronism, slack off at every opportunity because they can and because they know I'm the American kid with something to prove. So, they relax and let me perform.

"Why you come here, do this?" they ask me in broken English.

I don't answer them; I just grab another table end and wait for one of them to finish a cigarette and grab the other. They don't need to know my reasons.

Darla cradles me, limp in her hand, and sings along to the Billie Holiday tape in the player she'd put in the middle of the living room. She rocks back and forth when she does this. It annoys me, but she gets me stoned enough so that I don't mind much. Plus, the pot and wine help relax my muscles. Two songs later, I've almost fallen asleep on the old rug, but I feel Darla squeezing me. Despite my brain telling me to sleep, my cock is still young and has a mind of its own. The blood begins to return despite my efforts to detour it.

"Can you get it up again?" She squeezes.

We get off of the rug, our ashes and wine and stain of memory left on it, and walk up the winding staircase. The stairs are worn and creak, and she turns back to tell me her parents are sleeping, so I should be quiet.

Her room is at the top of the stairs to the right. She raises a single finger to her lips and points to the end of the hallway. *Be quiet, right. Got it.* Inside her room is a four-poster bed with billowing drapery, a full-sized oval vanity mirror, and several dressers, each of which is worth more than a year or two of my salary, I've no doubt.

"Shit, we forgot the wine downstairs," I realize.

She's already naked in the bed, her long black hair splayed out, her legs spread. Her hands grab the posts on the headboard. This pose, with the inviting bud between her legs, her arm muscles flexed to pull up the skin, makes her breasts perfectly round orbs. This is something that I want to imprint on my brain, something that I want to be able to recall at any instant of any future day, but I know there will be a hazy memory of this, nothing more.

"Leave it. Just come here. I want it now," she says. Her breasts ebb with her breath. She really does look beautiful—a black-maned Greek sculpture with solid white curves. I decide to leave the wine.

Darla likes it hard enough to put the thick oak headboard into the wall, hard enough to make her bite and moan so that I have to cover her mouth, but not hard enough that it actually hurts. She likes me to pull her hair, but not too hard. We go for a long time, especially the second time around—thanks to the wine and pot.

Finally, she tells me I need to roll off; she's getting sore. I haven't come a second time, but I'm too tired even to work out an eloquent way to ask her to finish me off with her mouth. She's asleep inside of three minutes. I lie there staring at the ceiling, unable to sleep. The pot's got me spinning tonight. I'm too tired;

4

I'm wearing myself out. But I see no reason to stop. I'm in a big, sterile museum with a beautiful girl I barely know, a dirty rug, and an unspent payload. That's not an inventory list that screams happiness. I don't know what it screams, but whatever the word or sentiment is, it is a forceful whisper that sucks the air out of my chest and weighs on me like an invisible weight. I look at the clock. I have to get up and go to work in two hours. I've drunk away any conscience for one more night; the immediate goal of getting from one day to the next has been achieved. The ceiling continues to spin as the sun comes up, and my balls begin to ache from being full, but everything else seems empty.

I drag ass all day at work. Hangovers and moving furniture don't mix. We are up and down narrow staircases with love seats and book collections. Nobody wants to get the box of books when it comes to moving, so I make sure to grab it every time, just to show the LNs that I'm not making light of what puts food on their table. It gets me just enough respect for them not to leave me behind when they pull out at 6:00 every morning.

Around midday, my energy spent, I drop a boxful of a major's cassette tapes. The box rips, so they scatter down several flights of stairs, shattering—*Tsshhacktsshhacktsshhack!*—all the way down.

My co-worker LNs find this amusing, of course.

"You tired, Ami boy? Look at the *reech* Ami boy, drunk and stink like whore!" They're enjoying it. Can't say I blame them.

"Not too tired to kick your ass," is the best I can manage for a response, which only makes them laugh harder. Let them have their day. I'll be back with my chip on my shoulder tomorrow.

The shower after work feels better than losing my virginity. I try to take an extra long one, but the hot water runs out about ten minutes in. Unpaid gas bill. Just like the phone. Just like the rent. At least I have electricity for tonight; lights and music and ice for the drinks are all I need to make it through.

With no TV to watch, since the cable bill is also unpaid, I take a drink out to my porch. The crickets buzz, and it's humid. Somebody is grilling hot dogs. A breeze tells me it's going to rain later. I walk back to the turntable and flip through some records, deciding on the *Eight Miles High* seven inch. It is feeling like a Husker Du evening—fuzzy with a dash of pop sadness.

I plop the needle into a groove and settle back on the porch with my feet up and a rum and Coke in my hand. The breeze begins to thin out the humidity a little, and the mosquitoes scatter in it like those shards from the exploding cassette cases, specks of malaria carriers sent to a pond and out of harm's way. Dusk brings out the after-work joggers, dog walkers, and those with less productive pursuits: the drinkers. I toast into the air—to myself and everything around—grateful for the blessing of a nice, quiet evening of individual achievement, mine underway and ready to be enjoyed.

Several blissful drinks later, a brand-new Acura pulls in front of my apartment and Darla gets out. My instinct is to retract my toast to the evening—both *quiet* and *individual* having been stripped from my goals for it; now it is left only with the designation "evening." Darla waves as she walks up the sidewalk, her store-ripped jeans and Che Guevara T-shirt fitting perfectly on her curved frame. Sometimes, Darla wants to be on the outside so much it makes me swell with delight at her efforts, because I can see through the thin layer of carefully planned rebelliousness. In high school, I would have ridiculed her; now, wiser, I find it cute. I've always found girls who *wished* they could be bad much more endearing than *actual* bad girls, maybe because they were less of a lost cause or maybe because I thought they might not be gone enough to try to save me—if I wanted saving.

I fix us drinks and reset the needle on the turntable. We sit there looking out at the trees and cobblestone. It is quiet out there, but the stereo interrupts the quiet just enough for us to hear it on the porch. I lean back in my chair and put my feet up again; Darla follows suit.

"Husker Du, nice," she says and then grimaces at her first sip of the drink. *"Gaah!* Is this straight up?"

"That's how I roll, baby."

"It's disgusting."

"It's the quickest way to drink away your conscience."

"Why would I want to do that?"

"Shots would be quicker, I guess," I sidetrack myself.

"Sometimes you're fucking weird," she blurts, but I don't mind.

We both light up smokes and listen to Bob Mould scream his guts out as the sun finally sets and the breeze dies. It's purple and blue and orange in a gradient, as if the horizon were candlelit.

Thinking along that line, I set a candle on the porch table, and we fight off the returning mosquitoes with our cigarettes. A last jogger and dog walker go by, most people in the neighborhood having now gone in to prepare for a meal or television as the dark has set.

"You know who we remind me of?" I ask her.

"Wait, let me guess—a Norman Rockwell painting? If they had multiple piercings in those," she says. "I mean, look at this neighborhood; it has Rockwell all over it."

"Yeah, yeah. The neighborhood suits me. It's the one thing I can afford—my own posh, run-down, termite-ridden cave. And, no, I wasn't thinking Rockwell, to answer your question. Have you seen *Repo Man?*"

"The movie? Emilio Estevez? Of course. Great movie... except for Emilio Estevez. Whatever happened to that guy anyway?"

"I dunno. But what we remind me of, in a way, we're the punk couple that robs stores. Except you're not black."

"Is this where I say, 'Let's go do some crimes'?"

"No, this is where I say, 'Let's get married and get a house with a white picket fence.' Only we don't die in this version."

She takes a drag off of her cigarette and then says, "If you love somebody, is it possible to just fuck them?"

"I wouldn't know," I say, wondering what the answer is. I'm not sure I've ever loved to begin with.

"Well, there you have it," she says. Damn, she is good.

Maybe we do die in this version, I think.

I stick with Husker Du and move on to *Warehouse Songs & Stories*. Darla has gotten through her first drinks and with a numbed mouth, no longer complains about my pours. The mosquitoes swirl around us as we sing "Charity, Chastity, Prudence, and Hope" at the top of our lungs until the candle runs out. The neighborhood takes no notice.

We wind up in bed. She lies there as she did last night—her white skin reflecting moonlight, legs spread and arms outstretched to me, her breasts globed crests worth following blindly into oblivion.

"Now," she says.

I crawl on top of her, and she locks me in with her legs. I go slow and press flush to her.

"*Oooohmm,*" she says.

"*Uhh,*" I say.

Slow. Quiet for the sake of quiet. We move and sweat, but I'm doing it how I want to do it for once: soft and gentle. My muscles, tired and sore, contract and expand, a slow therapy that dissipates the conscience and ache. I can smell her hair and her inviting bud's scent at the same time; it's a sweet summer evening and the crusades rolled into one. Her breathing increases. I've got my mouth on her neck and push in further, and I know I never want to leave there; I never want to stop this delicate battle.

"I love you," I say into her neck and then look up at her, still pushing in.

Her brow is furrowed.

"Don't say that to me now. It ruins it."

I feel the bud contract, and though the grip is a universe of feeling unto itself, I know its cause. It is not an invitation; it is expulsion.

I don't say anything; guilt is not a luxury I can focus on. Guilt is a rug you stain and leave behind.

I pick up the pace. I grab her hair. I go deeper, soft and gentle having run their course.

"*Oaaaahaah!*" she yells in ecstasy, and she has rejoined the delicate battle on her own terms.

I grunt also, but I've disassociated. I'm in the museum of Darla, and none of my art hangs on the walls. The crusade is over; the sweet summer evening has contracted malaria. I figure I'll just grab on for now and give her something to admire.

Tomorrow, I'll be back with my chip on my shoulder—focused, not scattered. You don't need to know my reasons, but I guess I've spilled that being saved wouldn't be so bad at all.

In Fifths and Packs

The days are sticky and humid. It's Florida in summer, and all you can do is sit, drink, and bake in the heat. So I sit on the hood of my car with my bottle and watch them work out their plans. They have it all figured out—blueprints to some meat-packing plant that doubles as a mob money-laundering facility. How inbreeds like this got information this good I don't know, but I can't ask questions. I am the dumb one here; I have to remember that. I'm the drunk, the village idiot. I count time by packs of cigarettes and fifths of rum. As long as my kidneys and lungs can hold out, I'm solid. I'm dying waiting for them to move on this job, but they just think I'm waiting to die, me and my pea brain and shot liver, which is exactly what I want them to think.

"Asshole!" P.W. shouts, his finger motioning me toward the three of them gathered around a Chevette. I peel my ass off of the hood of my car and walk over to them. P.W., Henry, and Jas, which is short for Jasper, all stare at me.

"Go to the store and get us more beer. We're out," P.W. says. P.W. is short for Pee Wee, a name that is true to his stature, but the man is also a powder keg of stupidity and violence. It does not take much to set Pee Wee off, and despite his size, years of lifting in the joint made him a brute to go with that low center of gravity.

"I can't," I say. "I'm drunk. I can't lose my license. I have work tomorrow."

"It's two blocks!" P.W. raises his arms in mock exasperation. "You can make it. Don't be a pussy!"

"I can't," I say.

I've never once driven to get them beer, always claiming work despite my constant drinking. Since I've been consistent about it, they don't really bat an eye when I tell them no. Not once had they thought of telling me to walk.

"But your job is a fucking ID checker, man," P.W. persists, referring to my imaginary job as an ID checker at Sam's Club. I have no job, but my income means aren't important to them, yet. So I lied.

"It's a job, and it's important to me," is all I say, and I just stand there, I hope looking stupid.

I guess it works, because a few seconds later, P.W. says, "Ah, fuck it, he's useless. Henry, go get some damn beer." P.W. throws some cash at him, and Henry hops in the car and leaves. The car pulls out, and the blueprint comes off of the hood, drifting back and forth before settling at my feet.

"Be careful, jackass!" P.W. yells at Henry, who is already speeding off.

I look down at the blueprint. Whatever they are planning isn't going to work; these dumb motherfuckers couldn't even read blueprints. They have half of their paths traced through vents and solid walls. I try not to laugh, but it doesn't work.

"Look at Jimmy boy there!" P.W. says to Jas, as he starts pointing and laughing at me.

"He ain't never seen nothin' like that! He thinks it's one of them mazes on the kids' mats at McDonald's!"

They both start laughing.

I look up and keep laughing too, making sure they think it's with them and not at them.

A minute later, Barbara, P.W.'s wife, appears at the screen door.

"Don't you boys make fun of Jimmy no more—quit it!"

Everyone stops laughing, but it turns into one of those under-the-breath chuckles that works itself back up, so once Barb has shut the screen door, they begin pointing at me and laughing harder, which only makes me smile and hopefully look even dumber.

A fifth and a pack, it must be 8:00 or 9:00 p.m. Jas has taken off, and that leaves me, Henry, Barb, and P.W. drinking in the carport. We have all been drinking for hours. Henry and P.W. had shared a jail cell for a few years and have that cellmate bond, but Henry also sleeps with P.W.'s wife every time P.W.'s back is turned. So I know the fight is coming at some point. The question is when?

"Ge' me a beer," Barb says to P.W. as she pops a Valium and puts her false teeth into a tumbler of gin and tonic she has set beside her on the step in the carport to soak. P.W. opens the screen door and steps in to grab the beer. Barb looks at Henry and bares her gums; Henry winks back at her and rubs his crotch.

"Later, baby, later," he says.

Nobody even looks at me. I just sit there and take a swig from my bottle, as I stare off across the lawn pretending not to notice.

"D'you t'ink you can pull't off?" Barb asks.

"The job? No problem," Henry says to her. Henry is wiry, all muscle and tan from a lifetime in Florida and years of hard work and hard time. His slimness is deceptive; when he and P.W. fight, Henry usually wins. He is strong and slippery and quick. I'll have to remember that.

I look back toward them. Staring off too long would be suspicious.

"What are you guys talking about?" I ask. "You guys finally got jobs?"

Henry laughs, and Barb covers her mouth, trying not to spit out gin.

"Yeah, Jimmy, we got jobs. That's why we're celebrating."

"Oh," I say. "All right!"

As I say this, P.W. comes out and asks what's going on. Henry shares what was just said with P.W., and he goes into a small laughing fit as well. After he's finished laughing, he looks at me, and I smile. His face turns serious, and he says, "You know, he sounds dumb sometimes, but he's too quiet. It's them quiet ones'r smart."

Everybody looks at me for a moment. I maintain a poker face, but inside, I'm wondering whether they've figured me out. I gauge whether I can take Henry and P.W. bare-handed and try to decide whom I should take out first. I figure Barb isn't much of a threat outside of a frying pan to the back of the head. I suppose it could get ugly; these guys could take me if I couldn't get inside to my gear fast enough.

But instead, they all start laughing.

"Asshole!" P.W. says, repeating his inventive nickname for me, and they burst into another fit of laughter.

In between snorts of breath, Henry adds, "Yeah, them quiet ones you gotta watch out for!" which makes them all laugh harder.

I go ahead and laugh along with them. My muscles relax, and my grip on the brick beside me loosens.

What I'm waiting for, at least this evening, takes another hour and a half to transpire. Everybody is much drunker now.

I'm leaning back on the hood of my car, which is parked alongside the carport, not inside of it where the other three are. P.W. goes in through the screen door to take a piss, and Henry takes the opportunity to sidle up to Barb, who is managing to weave even though she's seated on the step. I hear a zipper sound and then look over and see Barb's head moving back and forth into Henry's crotch. The sound of Barb's gums slurping makes my stomach turn a little, until I hear the toilet flush inside, which helps drown it out. That means P.W. will be stepping back outside momentarily. I can't have these people trying to kill each other right now, so I drop my bottle onto the concrete.

"Dammit! Nice job, Jimmy!" I yell to myself.

Henry pulls away and zips up just seconds before P.W. appears in the screen door carrying more beer. Barb is finishing wiping her mouth as he hands her a can. Then he leans down and kisses her, and over P.W.'s shoulder, I can see Henry wink at Barb and I can see that she is looking at him. P.W. pulls back just in time to see the direction of Barb's gaze.

There is a second of discomfort as everyone wonders whether P.W. is bright enough to connect the dots.

"What. The. Fuck!" P.W. says, looking between Barb and Henry and then at me, but I leave a dumb quarter smile on my face that says I have no idea what is goin' on.

"What, *what, what* the fuck?" Henry says, trying, perhaps, some type of new Jedi mind trick. I have to admit, the triple repetition is an intriguing ploy; it does make P.W. pause for a second, but he recovers.

"What's this? No...wait, I suspected this shit for a while!" He screams at Barb and then turns to Henry. "*You?*" He looks back at Barb and then back to Henry. "You two? How long? All those years locked up! We're brothers! You mother*fuck*—"

P.W. swings. Henry can't duck in time, despite his deftness, and Pee Wee catches him with a glancing but powerful blow. Henry slides down the front of the parked Chevette but picks himself up quickly. I have to admit I'm impressed at his ability to recover so quickly.

Henry has his hands half up in defense and is half crouched.

"Listen now, P.W., ain't nothing going on here. I got no idea what you mean. Me and Barb are just friends. She's your woman."

P.W. takes another swing but misses, and they rotate, circling each other now.

"Fuck you, Henry! I know this…what this is," P.W. says, his inebriation showing. "All those years, we survived. We had each other's back!" P.W. turns his arm to show a tattoo. "Remember this, motherfuck? Brothers! You been fucking your brother's wife!"

Henry is slightly more intelligent than P.W. and decides to try a diversion tactic.

"Ask Jimmy! He's too dumb to lie! Wouldn't he know? Jimmy, Jimmy, tell P.W. Is anything going on?" As Henry turns toward me and away from P.W., his eyes widen and he brings one hand across his throat to tell me if I say anything about the gumjob a few minutes ago, he'll kill me.

I choose to say nothing. Finally, P.W. asks me, "Jimmy, you seen anything up with these two? You seen them kissing or anything? Looking at each other?"

I shake my head. "No, P.W. We're all friends here. I'm all out of rum. You have any beer?"

P.W. throws up his hands in disgust. Barb takes the opportunity to put her teeth back in and goes inside to grab beer.

Henry looks at me from the side of his face, but I can't read the look.

"Don't you try no shit with my wife," P.W. says to Henry.

"Brother, I would never do that," Henry says to P.W. and pats him on the back.

"I got beer for y'all," Barb says, appearing at the screen door.

I am taking notes on all of these rednecks and saying nothing.

I decide not to sleep in the house. My car is safer, and it makes me look odder, which can only help in case Henry thinks something is already off with me. Plus, it gives me some time by myself to figure some things out.

The plan they have is completely ridiculous; they will wind up with nothing, and one or all of them will get shot. That will not be good for me, so I need to help them out somehow. I need to help them with their blueprint issues; I need at least one of them to get back from the job safely, with the cash.

Jasper, I am also a little concerned about. He's not around the house as much and does not have the history that P.W. and Henry have together. I haven't been able to gather much on Jas at all and don't know quite where he fits into the picture, especially with his German accent. He's certainly not a part of their regular crew. It's possible that the job was his idea, and he just needed some dumb muscle. It would explain the knowledge of the plant and the blueprints and using two borderline-retarded ex-cons for a score that was sure to bring down mob heat on their heads. At the same time, the score is mob money, so it will be a good payday. I don't even think P.W. and Henry have thought that far ahead. Jas is an unknown—a *foreign*—entity, a variable.

18

I am having problems with Jas. If P.W. and Henry got knocked off during the job, Jas most assuredly will not come back here afterward. I need to make sure that happens somehow.

In the morning, I crack open a fifth and open the back driver's side door of my car. I pour half of the fifth out and pour flat soda in to fill the rest of the bottle. Then I walk into the house.

Barbara is making toast. At the kitchen table, Henry is holding an ice pack to his head where P.W. punched him. P.W. is in the living room watching cartoons. I sit at the kitchen table and take a swig from the bottle.

"Morning," I say.

"Fuck you, Jimmy," Henry says.

I look around. I don't see the blueprints anywhere. Barb places toast on the table, and as she does so, I grab a pen from the mail holder.

"Where's the maze, Barb?" I ask her, giving her my best earnest-kid look. It works on the women, but guys never fall for it. I make sure Henry is still wallowing in his ice pack when I pull the face on Barb.

"What, hon?" she says.

"The maze. I know a better way than they found."

"Maze...oh! The maze!" Barb looks at Henry, who looks up at her from under his ice pack. The two of them look over at P.W. in the recliner in the living room.

"What?" he shouts to them, muting what sounds like Wile E. Coyote falling off of a cliff.

"Where's the blueprints?" Henry asks him.

After P.W. and Henry have their obligatory argument about how stupid asshole drunk Jimmy shouldn't be allowed near their precious material, they finally decide that if I use pencil, I can mark on the blueprint.

"Okay, Jimmy, show us what you mean," Barb says unfolding the blueprint in front of me.

I hold the pencil ready and then take a swig of rum and Coke, which nearly makes me retch. This diet is killing me.

I begin marking the route they should take on the print, commenting as I go, being sure to call vents "bad caves" and doors they won't be able to access "back to beginning" bars. They seem to buy it. I've planned out the best path for them to take through the plant.

P.W. and Henry stare at it for a minute, unsure. Then they both get it.

"Holy shit," Henry says from beneath his melting ice bag.

"Holy shit," P.W. repeats, left with few other vocabulary options. "It's them quiet ones..."

"Dumb shit Jimmy is Rain Man!" Henry says.

"You're going into the maze, right?" I ask them.

"Yeah, yeah, Jimmy. There's a prize at the end. We're prize hunting."

"Well..." I say, letting it hang and then also letting my eyes wander off toward the ceiling fan.

"Well what, Jimmy? Tell us? We can give you some of the prize! It's...chocolate. Chocolate...and...drinks. All you can drink for a whole night for free! Whatever you want."

I pull my eyes back to them. "Well, when you win a prize, you have to go on a trip. Everybody who wins. Where are you going? Are you taking me with you?"

The table is silent. Henry, P.W., and Barb all look at each other.

"You know, Jimmy, that's a good question. We need to figure out where we're going to go. So why don't you take your… bottle…and go out to the carport, and we'll come out there and let you know where we all will go if Henry and P.W. win the prize, okay?" Barb says.

I give them a low-IQ skeptical look and then say, "Okay!"

I can hear them talking inside from the open side window.

"That kid may be dumb as a motherfucking rock, but he has a point. How do we make sure nobody runs off with all the dough?"

"We can't trust each other?"

"We can't trust Jas; that's for damn sure. Who knows what that Kraut bastard has up his sleeve?"

"Look, I trust you two, but until all three—I mean four of us…okay, five if we're taking Jimmy—until we're all sipping piña coladas on the beach somewhere together, I'm not relaxing. So, I want a plan. I want to make sure everybody—and I mean every-motherfucking-body—comes back to the same spot before skipping the country. How do we do that?"

"Jimmy's seen our faces and the blueprints; dumb shit or not, we have to take him, at least for a while; we can lose him later. Hang on," I hear Barb say.

There's a bit of silence. Then there is no more talking at all. I raise my head to try to hear if they are moving around and talking, but I hear nothing. Had I made a noise outside of the window? I look around—nobody to the sides, no noises I can make out at all. I start to move toward the car. If I get caught eavesdropping, it will blow everything. Every step I take seems to make a loud crunch in the brittle Florida grass, and even the hum of the air conditioner can't help drown me out. I move as fast as I can to the hood of my car, assume the position, and take a swig from my bottle.

"Jimmy?"

I lower the bottle, and I am so surprised to see all three of them there that I spit out the vile rum and day-old Coke concoction right into Henry's face and shirt.

"Sorry," I say to him. "You scared me!"

I hold up my hands to show them I'd been shocked, but everyone seems to want to be nice to me right now. Henry even lets his scowl turn into a smile.

"Jimmy, Jimmy, it's okay," Barb says. P.W. echoes her statement. Even Henry begrudgingly admits it's okay.

"Jimmy, we need you to do something for us," Barb says in a very saccharine voice. I raise an eyebrow, giving her a quizzical look that says, "I don't know about what you're going to ask me here, but I might have also just shit my drawers for no reason."

"Yes?" I say, drawing the word out so that I come across as the idiot pretending to be smart. Behind Barb, P.W. lets the slightest snicker go through his pursed lips. I can tell it's taking everything he has to hold it in, and the more I notice it, the more it is making me want to laugh, so I make sure to keep my eyes square on Barb.

"Jimmy, we need you to hold on to everybody's beach pass, because if we win the prize, we're all going to the beach!" Barb says, very excitedly toward the end, as if this were a game show and I'd won something other than passport watch duty. Barb hands me a stack of passports.

"Here's the beach passes. Keep them safe, Jimmy!"

"Okay!" I say, trying to mimic her false excitement.

"Keep them in a secret place, and don't tell anybody where they are until everyone is back from the maze with the prizes, okay?"

I quickly look through the passports. "Okay. But where's Jas's? What if he wins? He can't go to the beach?"

Everyone deflates for a moment and looks at each other. For a second, I think they are all going to huddle, but Barb speaks up.

"We'll get his, okay? You'll hold his too."

"Oh, okay. Because I'd like all of us to go to the beach."

"Yes, Jimmy, we all want to go to the beach," Barb says.

Then everybody's act shrugs off, and they disappear into the house. I find a place to put their passports and wait for game time.

Jas shows up an hour before they are to leave for the heist.

He doesn't like the changes they had made—which, of course, I had really made, but maybe only Jasper, the Teutonic question mark, has picked up on that.

I am on the hood of my car, counting packs of cigarettes and sips of rum, when he cracks out of the screen door and storms up to me.

"Vhat is your game, kid?" he asks me, putting his face right up to mine. I lean back a little on the hood, peel the part of my ass off of it that is uncomfortable and set it back down, and then return my face to within an inch of his.

"What's your game, kid?" I repeat to him.

He doesn't know how to react to this, which is the point.

"Vhat kind of bull-*Sheize* are you trying to pull over our eyes? Who are you? Vhere do you come from?"

The rest of the household has rushed outside as well, and they are near the car. I point to them and say, "I got a job! It's an ID checker. I don't want to fight. I lose my job if I fight; they said so."

"Zhat's not a fuck-king answer, *arschloch*!" Jas spews, slamming his fist into the hood of my car. I make sure not to flinch. Only somebody cognizant of danger would flinch.

"I can't lose my license," I say, looking down at the hood. "I have to work tomorrow."

"Oh Jesus H. Fuck-king Chriszt *mit zhis*," Jas says, spins around in a rage, and finally stares at me from a few feet away. I stare back, but dimly, and take a swig from my bottle. Losing his temper is starting to make Jas revert back to his father tongue.

"Jas, it's just Asshole. Give him your damn passport, and let's go. We meet back here anyway; that's the plan," P.W. says.

Poor P.W., I think, *he has no idea.*

Jas is left with no choice but to play the game my way.

"Fuck-king *Scheizkopf*," Jas says and throws his passport at me. It hits me forcibly in the chest. *Nice throw.* I have the distinct feeling I just ruined Jasper's plan A.

"All right, let's go," he says to Henry and P.W., and I wonder if I'll ever see those dimwits again.

Barb waves good-bye to the three of them in the carport as if they were headed off to church.

Barb has to go first.

It's too bad; she's kind of nice, in a fuck-your-husband's-best-friend kind of way.

I have a box of two hundred garbage bags planted behind the house. They are the lawn variety, these bags: large and black. For a moment, I wonder if Sam's Club and the police will be able to track the purchase of the box to Sal Moss, whom I chopped up and left in his own septic tank two months ago.

I grab the box and head into the house. I mark each window and door and then grab some duct tape I had stored under the sink and begin taping up every possible exit point and any point that was visible from the outside. I make it to the living room before Barb comes out of her gin-and-Valium haze long enough to question what I'm doing.

"Jimmy, what are you doing?"

"Oh, just playing hide-and-seek, Barb," I say.

"Huh," she says and stands there a moment. I use that time to tape up the large picture window.

"But it's kind of dark, don't you think?"

"That's the point of hide-and-seek."

"Yeah, Jimmy, but, I mean, what?"

I laugh. "That was almost as good as Henry's triple 'what.'"

"Huh?"

"Exactly."

"I don't like this, Jimmy. What is going on?"

"Why don't you help me play hide-and-seek and tape some of this up?"

"Hide-and-seek for who, Jimmy?" Barb has her arms crossed now and is starting to rub them nervously.

"For everybody. Just grab some tape and a bag and put it on a window."

"I...don't think I want to do that. You need to stop this now, Jimmy. We are going to be leaving in an hour or two. We need to pack up. You have to stop this."

I look at her for a minute. I hesitate because it's almost not fair; she has no idea. At the same time, she has every clue. As I see it, this is the point in the horror movie where she should be screaming at herself on the screen to get the fuck out of the house. But no, she needs to stand here and rationalize. I find this is typical of most people, surprisingly.

"Barb. Look, I'm sorry, but you're not going anywhere. None of you are. Nothing personal, but when you fell into this job months ago—and I have to admit that I am a little disappointed you are all so unmotivated it took you this long to finally get your shit together, but, I digress—when you fell into this job, I fell into your lives. And my job is to make the score and make damned sure none of you ever see the light of day again. Because if you do, I can't make my next score. Because my next score will come off of whatever information one of your boys gives me before they die. And believe me, they will die, long, excruciatingly painful deaths. I am in the robbery business, but I am also in the torture business. The difference between me and most operations is: I am a one-man operation. It's best that way. Low overhead and all that."

Barb just stands there rubbing her arms nervously. She either cannot accept the truth, or has, and cannot move.

"Barb, I can kill you quickly, and I can even promise to kill your husband—hell, even Henry—quickly, if you can just give me information on who tipped you to this job. Because that will help lead me to my next job. Before I came here, I did a job with a man named Sal Moss. Do you know him?"

Barb nods her head yes.

"He's no longer with us. His way out was not pleasant. He chose not to give me the information that I wanted…and yet, here I am anyway. Do you understand?"

Barb does manage to move to the couch and sit down but keeps her arms crossed. She seems to be shaking a little.

"Barb, if you shut down on me, you're useless. It would make me keep you for last. That could prolong your life for a little while...while you get to hear the others. Or maybe you don't know anything anyway and I can just kill you now. Your friend Sal chose the long way around. He did a large job over in Palm Beach, and I was there before—and after—as I am here. Before Sal, I did a job with someone who gave me Sal's name and said Sal had a job brewing. And so on. It's what I do."

Barb just sits there, staring at the wall, so I continue, "But Sal just didn't want to talk. I guess he valued his time in with Henry and Pee Wee there. The brothers' tattoos or whatever it is they all have. Those are some real winners you got by the way."

I finish taping up the living room.

"So, Barb. Give me a name. I'll even fix up a Valium job for you that you won't even feel. Otherwise, you're going to get the Sal Moss treatment. It's fun, but time-consuming, all that torture. So, tell me, do you want to go to the beach...or, would you like the alternative?"

Barb looks up to me at the mention of her own previous lie. I'm sure she is contemplating calling me a monster or something equally trite, but to her credit, she chooses not to.

"They don't tell me names," she says quietly.

"Then it's no sand and surf for you, sister."

She doesn't say anything, but she'll be screaming soon enough.

The Chevette pulls into the carport about a quarter pack after I set Barb up. There is muffled yelling and the scuffle of shoes, and then the screen door opens and shuts. The three robbers race into the kitchen.

"Barb!" I hear P.W. yell, which is immediately followed by, "What. The. Fuck?"

"Mein Gott," Jasper whispers.

Henry vomits.

I am behind them, barricading the door. They don't hear me. They are looking at Barb's limbless torso presented on the corner of the kitchen table, like a hood ornament. I figured that was fitting, but I doubt they appreciate the touch of irony.

Her severed head and limbs strung up across the other kitchen doorways serve well enough to block the exits; they won't try to go through those, at least at first. I move from the door toward their backs, machete in my hand. There is a bag in Henry's hand—I'm assuming it's full of cash—and a side of beef in P.W.'s hand. They actually took a side of beef from the plant. When were they planning on eating it?

Jas is staring slack-jawed at Barb's dead tits on the table. He is gone, out of commission, mind in shock. He'll be easy to interrogate as long as I can keep him speaking English, and something tells me that he has names of good contacts, names that could help me land some good jobs, maybe even international jobs. I wonder for a second if my own passport has expired. Jas was in for a long night, the longest of them all. Hell, he might break my record.

Henry is still vomiting, so I turn to Pee Wee first, the scrapper with the strength of a bull and the low center of gravity.

I motion with my finger.

"It's Asshole Jimmy!" I smile, and that side of beef hits the kitchen tile with a dull, thick thud.

More James Dean

"Sitting in the dark, pretending to be all alone again?" Faith asks me, dropping her purse at the front door and kicking off her sandals under the mail table. I get the trademark frown from her and the hands on the waist, representing defiance, but I find the stance incredibly attractive, as it accentuates her hips.

"I *am* alone," I state the fact.

"But you've got more friends than God," she says while grabbing a beer from the fridge. She turns on a light in the foyer on her way to the desk where I am sitting.

"I don't understand why you do this to yourself. You could be at five different happy hours across town, tying one on with someone or, God forbid, trying to meet a good woman."

"Yeah, that's *exactly* what I need right now."

"You'd be surprised. So, let me guess, you're sulking again? What is it this time?"

She sits in the foldout chair beside the desk where, admittedly, I am sulking. But I like to sulk.

"Sitting here is one of life's few free luxuries," I tell her. "Do I need an excuse? I'm just enjoying some me time."

"You have so much '*me*' time I don't see how you manage to enjoy it. Besides, it can't be healthy."

"*Me* time is better than 'other people' time, most of the time."

She just humphs and picks a cat up off the floor. I light up a smoke, and she looks at me and then at my glass.

"Tell me you aren't starting with rum?" She frowns again.

"And ending with it," I say and exhale smoke, as if I'd said something that meant anything at all. Here in my chair, I am the causeless rebel of shut-ins.

"Sometimes I fucking hate you." She sighs.

I'm renting an apartment to surround my chair in the dark. Six years in the same place, and it is still standing. Somehow, so am I. At least while I am sober. I have enough to buy drinks and gamble and treat the women decently, but I do mostly sit alone, I drink more than gamble, and the women are few. I spoil myself by not spoiling myself with the problems of others. I do prefer to keep the apartment dimly lit. Faith sees "dark"; I see soft yellow light. The calming yellow helps me forget about those fluorescents in my corporate cubicle, blasting their soul-cooking white rays from the ceiling and destroying my circadian rhythms.

She just likes to point out what a hermit I've become for her own amusement.

"I'm just busting your balls," she says, "because I can."

"I think you're just jealous," I joke.

"Maybe a little."

"Really?" I look at my surroundings. "Of what? I drink, I write, I rent, I work—sometimes. My car breaks down. Raccoons live on my porch. Roaches crawl out of my drains. And despite your assessment of my number of friends, I am alone. As you can see..." I grandly wave my hand around the empty, yellow space of the apartment.

"I knew you were sulking!" she says gleefully. "But sure, you're right. Of course, there are the advantages." She takes a large swig of her beer as the cat purrs in her lap.

I laugh. "Advantages?"

"Sure, advantages! You have nobody to answer to but yourself. You can do whatever you want, whenever you want. Why wouldn't most people be jealous of that? That's a precious commodity for most people."

"For most people," I say.

The cat sees a squirrel in a tree through the window and bolts from Faith's lap. She brushes a few cat hairs off and continues as if I hadn't said anything.

"What you have is yours—your time is yours; your space is yours—and you spend it like this…" She imitates my hand wave, covering the apartment, ending with me slouching in a chair with my drink. I get her point.

"If personal time is so important to people, why would I leave all this…" I make another arc with my arm, "…to infringe on their—how did you put it? Their *precious commodity*? Plus," I add, "people always pack too much goddamn drama."

"I think you need a little drama in your life. Quit the Thoreau routine and shoot for more James Dean."

"I think I need another drink in my life," I say, squinting at the empty glass in my hand.

"Sometimes you are impossible."

"No," I respond smugly, "I'm rational. It depends on how you look at it, but I make sense. At least one way of sense…making. That didn't make sense, did it?"

"A few more of those rums, you'll be making none at all." She shakes her head.

"That also depends upon your perspective." I exhale, making a few smoke rings.

She convinces me to at least get some fresh air, so we transfer the drinks to the porch, light up smokes, and kick back. My routine of sitting, drinking, and writing for long periods of time does leave a film of smoke on the walls that is easy to forget about if you are immersed in the cloud of it all. Faith calls it a cocoon, but I like to think of it as a cloud; an atmosphere of swirling smoke like one would find in any good dive bar—without the people. It's easy enough to imagine the characters; dive bar clientele is the same anywhere you go.

The squirrel from before darts across the telephone line in front of the second-floor porch. Maybe he's running from the blaring radios whizzing by in the cars of those who are getting home late from work and have families to tend to. Or maybe he's running home to a family of his own. But we, on the porch, are in our own microcosm, separated from the rush and the telephones.

"I've always liked your place, even though I give you shit about it being a mole hole. It feels safe here," she says into a glass of newly poured wine.

"It is cozy." I nod in agreement. "Same thing: cozy, safe."

"Not really." She smiles. "Safe is good. But too much cozy makes aging, balding, drunken shut-ins soft." She chuckles and pats my beer belly.

I laugh along and stick my belly out as far as I can. "Yeah, but if you're going to do something, do it all the way. This gut has taken a lot of work to perfect, baby!"

She laughs and then says, "I know something I'd like to do all the way." She leaves her eyes on me and then quickly moves them to the cat at the screen door. She scratches the screen with her nails, and the cat tries to playfully bite them through the screen and then whines at her for teasing it.

I am awkwardly quiet for a moment. Her come-on is a surprise, but I like it. We've never been intimate, not that the potential isn't there for it. We just always seemed to have that friendship that is content to be flirty. As I think about it, it is a little odd maybe that we haven't moved to the bedroom; we drink and talk all night in a dark apartment, and there is a safe, cozy comfort in her company. I think about what she said earlier and realize that though we are in a cocoon on Thoreau's little pond, she wants to share it with a leather jacket on and a cigarette hanging out of her mouth.

A few radios and whizzing cars later, I can feel the rum kicking in, ounces of courage being fed into my veins. I catch myself staring over at Faith—at her full-cup breasts that aren't too large, at her flat, tan belly, at the shape of her thighs beneath the jeans. Her straight, brown hair covers half of her face as she stares out in front of us at the rooftops of houses, and though I don't know what she's thinking, I know that I *could* know if I asked. That is cozy, safe.

I let the courageous liquor take my shot.

"I want to sleep with you tonight."

"Okay," she says without even averting her eyes from the rooftops, as if she'd expected it all along.

"You know," she continues from her own thoughts, "all of these sloped roofs on all of these houses, what do they hide? I mean, who lives under them? What are their stories? Do you ever think about that? How many lives, stories, we will never be a part of—so much unknown, right in your neighbor's house..." she trails the thought off with a look back at the rooftops.

"Sure, I've thought that before. Like, when driving into a city. You are on the highway, and all of these buildings start showing up on the horizon, and you just have to think—how many people; how much heartbreak; how much love; how many intersecting destinies, missed connections, unnoticed coincidences? And all of those seemingly inconsequential stories, how amazing it all is. And part of you wants to know them all, somehow. The stories, not the people. I don't like people. Not that it keeps me from being captivated at the same time."

"I know what you mean." She nods. "But how about perfect stories? Are there those who made out all right? Even within our area here, how many people worked out all right? Or is every story...broken, somehow flawed? Are there crying mothers or abandoned children or worried fathers who can't pay the mortgage?"

I think about this for a bit, smoking my cigarette. Then I think, *What about Faith and me? Could we work out all right?* Maybe she was wondering the same thing—after we sleep together, will our story break? Reveal a flaw?

A car races by, someone on the way home to family, late for dinner or their favorite TV show. There is no sign of the squirrel.

"I think our story could be perfect," I say.

"Sometimes I fucking hate you," she says.

She means this in a good way.

Despite popular perception, hermits do have plenty of things to keep themselves busy. There's more drink; there's writing; there's playing an instrument; and of course, there's sulking. Too drunk to play the guitar and too cozy to write, I just sit on my rented porch that everybody and God wanted a part in, according to Faith. Faith, who has been sitting at my side for well over an hour now, just stares at rooftops.

"Are you still wondering about all of those random lives out there?" I ask her.

"Not really. I'm waiting for you to make a move so we can go to bed," she says without averting her eyes from the sloped, random rooftops.

The sex changes nothing, and yet it changes everything.

"Why did we wait so long to do this?" I do finally ask, though it isn't quite a question, it's more of a statement.

She doesn't say anything, curled up against me. I decide to answer my own question. "I guess I'm ready for a little less me time and more *us* time."

"That's my James Dean," she purrs, stretching her arm across my chest, like a cat putting a paw through the screen of a porch door, creating a small opening in its cocoon.

Spiked Bats and Leather Boots

Samantha constantly played a Mitch Hedberg CD in her car and would karaoke along with every joke of his. When she did this, she would laugh and bounce in her seat as if it were the first time she'd heard the joke, despite it being her thousandth listen. She would have a perma-grin, and her perky breasts would look so erect they could be dangerous weapons beneath her tight Mighty Mouse T-shirt. I missed pep like that; I missed unquestioning verve for life and the things it offered. That is what attracted me to Samantha—besides her toned dancer's body and natural beauty. So, I bought us tickets to see Mitch at the Improv. A few hundred bucks for a fun night out was no problem for me, and Samantha, plodding along at twelve an hour, was more than happy to accept the offer.

We'd been dating for a while. She wanted to take it slow, which I didn't mind at all. But, being experienced, I also knew Samantha's self-imposed resistance was waning when it came to sex, and I was willing to wait. To be honest, it was about sex just as much as it was sharing that verve for sex and for life and comedy and everything with her. It drew me to her, and with everything that she could bother focusing on at the time, she wanted me to want her. Being in her early twenties, she tended to distribute her attention amongst everything that came within range. Alternately, I chose to increasingly narrow my attentions and interests. I figured it either came with age, or I was just becoming boring, assuming the two are mutually exclusive.

We took a cab downtown on our way to the Hedberg show. It was a typically clear, warm Florida night. The calm, flat land melded with the calm skies; the temperature matched everything else with a dull lukewarm sedateness. This was every night in Florida; there's so much calm it can suck the willingness to move at all from you. But our cab ground on through, carrying what the climate strove to make immovable objects to our destination regardless of its will.

"Are the seats good?" she asked me as we turned onto Orange; the rows of bars were lit up, and people of every variety lined the sidewalks waiting to be let in. Clubs, pizza joints, sushi dens—they beckoned to the young and middle-aged to spite the imposing climate and inevitable boredom of a midstate city.

"Balcony, babe. Practically right on top of the stage. You could spit on him if you wanted to."

"I'd never do that!" she exclaimed with a frown and squinted eyes that should have proven me ridiculous for the thought.

I also knew there was the occasional miscommunication of intent between our age groups. I wouldn't spit on Mitch, though I am not a fan of people in general—so, I'm not saying I'm above it. If someone deserves it, they deserve it. Samantha, who found everyone and everything interesting on some level, made me realize how little faith in humanity I had. She had plenty to spare, and she believed people were inherently good. It was an unfortunate polarization we battled; like magnets, we repelled each other at ends, but set side by side, we were inseparable.

I can't say I wasn't looking forward to the sex. There are always things that surprise me with these younger women, but the most surprising is that they know how to *fuck*. I've dated several younger women, and the adage that older women are better in the sack because they know what they want is starting to turn on its head; it turns out it doesn't matter if you know what you want if you are willing to do anything. It makes me feel old to say it, but girls in "my day" were just starting to figure out what these girls now know early on. It's the sexual revolution all over again, except it's the dirty silent version; nobody's complaining about these girls knowing tricks—likely learned from older men—because everybody's in on the underground. They always told us in school that girls mature faster; it's either that or they develop an appreciation for money earlier. And now, maybe I am learning what they really meant, and maybe that is just one of society's dirty little secrets that I still have plenty to learn about. As Copeland says in *Love Is a Fast Song*, I shouldn't be angry that she wants my money, and she shouldn't be angry that I want her body. But that was simplifying everything and wasn't quite accurate. We shared *something*, though its meaning wasn't forever, and perhaps we both figured it was for now, for us, and along with everything, it was to learn.

"Drop us at Church Street Station," I told the cabbie.

People were already walking in a half daze, the late happy-hour crowd mixing with the crowd that drank at home before going out. The requisite fight between drunken assholes that people just sidestep on the way to their destinations happened as we stepped out of our cab.

Samantha found it fascinating; I just stepped past with barely a look. Samantha grabbed my arm, and we walked down the cobblestone heart of the small city, her long, beautiful boots click-clacking on the stones. She was slightly tipsy and leaned her head into my shoulder. It was times like this that almost made me think she cared for me, but that thought was fleeting and foolish, and I knew it. Music poured from the fronts of several bars, and girls paid to rope in customers trotted about in Catholic schoolgirl outfits that might as well be nothing.

"Hey, mister, want a shot for you and your lady?" I was asked, as the bouncers stood at the entrances with their clipboards.

Orlando was making a run at Manhattan, but it didn't have a clue how to pull it off. All I could see was the accosting of customers and then the belittling of those customers as they waited to get in to a club they were baited into entering. Samantha commented that maybe after the show, we could try one of the places out.

The comedy club was already packed. Some blonde in a tight black outfit that was part slut, part movie theater usher led us up the stairs to our seats. We were literally just about on top of the stage. Just a few feet below was the microphone that Mitch would deliver his material from. I ordered us a few drinks and some appetizers, and we watched the opening act: some dope from Tampa doing the redneck-hip routine, but he had some good pot jokes.

"I'm so excited!" she said. I smiled largely back at her. It was that energy, that *life* she had. It was so contagious. I couldn't remember the last thing I'd been truly excited about.

The Tampa redneck pot smoker finished his routine, and the crowd ate and drank until the lights went back down. People started yelling and clapping; Samantha, beside me, did also, so I figured what the hell, and joined in.

Some nobody introduced Hedberg, and he came onstage and cracked out a one-liner to get things started. I looked over at Samantha and saw she had both of her hands covering her mouth in an upside down "V" and her eyes were about to burst out of their sockets.

Hedberg was funny. Soon, we were all into the show, laughing and clapping. I kept the drinks coming out of pure habit and realized most of the crowd had stopped ordering, so the blonde in the tight outfit hovered around us.

I made sure to keep her busy; having your own private waitress should be taken advantage of. Several drinks later and halfway through his act, Samantha started doing *her* car act, saying every word along with Mitch from the balcony—and not quietly.

"Every book is a children's book if the kid can read!" he said, and sure enough, right along with him, Samantha yelled, "...if the kid can read!"

There was a second of silence, and then Mitch looked up at us. "Holy shit, I have an echo in here."

The spotlight settled on Samantha and me; I looked over at her mortified-yet-adulating face and realized she might as well have won a million dollars.

"Are you going to repeat everything I say the whole damn show?" he asked her, looking up into the spotlight.

She could only shake her head, "no," hands rising up to that toppled "V."

"All right," he said easily in his stoned voice and then turned back to the crowd.

"I got a fire alarm at home," he said, "but really, it's more like a nine-volt battery slowly draining. If you want to slowly get rid of your nine-volt batteries, then buy this circle." The crowd laughed, and Samantha's interruption was forgotten, but I could see on her face that she would never forget her moment in the spotlight with her idol. It made me happy to provide that, but there was still the boy inside of me that was stabbed with a little jealousy as the show finished; I felt pretty convinced that if she had the chance, she'd sashay backstage and fuck him with those knee-high black-leather boots on. Facing a peer entering your territory would be one thing; trying to fend off an idol would be futile.

Once the show was over, we decided to finish the night drinking at home rather than at one of the hostile bars, so I hailed another cab.

At home, I opened a bottle of wine while she changed and went into the bathroom for a minute. After lighting a few candles, I poured the wine, and she emerged from the bathroom, completely naked except for those boots.

I'm not sure what my face reflected, but I managed to ask, "Wine?"

She grinned back and shook her head no.

"Not yet."

Her brown hair was let down and left a paisley pattern on her shoulders and breasts, which were the most perfect breasts I had ever seen. I'd seen more than my fair share of incredible chests, but hers fully amazed me, no matter what my vantage point. Her dancer's ass and thighs supported those breasts and the boots below so naturally, I was immediately thinking about nothing else but corrupting every inch of her. She grabbed my hand and led me to the bedroom, and I followed willingly.

Afterward, we got to the rest of that bottle of wine, sipping it in bed to candlelight. Unlike some of the women I'd been with, she wasn't shy and left the sheets where they were rather than trying to pull them up in mock modesty. I appreciated her openness. After a while, a woman who still tries to cover up what is no longer a mystery starts to raise flags. Will the sex stop early? Is there a skeleton in some closet that requires her to be covered at all times? Besides, I was too old for that shit anyway.

"Good show tonight. He seemed to like you," I joked with her.

Her smile widened, and she drank from her wine, reliving the moment. I looked over, and those bronzing-worthy breasts heaved there, swirled by curls of brown hair, mostly still forward although we were propped up only partly on pillows.

"I'd totally do him," she said to me, still smiling.

When she said this, I wanted to tell her that was a great mood killer. I wanted to explain to her that no man ever wants to hear about a woman's infatuations if he's sleeping with her—no matter how starstruck or ridiculous, no matter how casual the relationship. That is not something that goes away with age. It's not necessarily jealousy; it's an inherited sense of ownership carried over from the Stone Age—even if the ownership was temporary.

But narrowing my attention, I figured, *Why not just focus on the moment?*

"That's nice," I replied to her, at a loss to say much else, though at the time, my mind was lost in thoughts of clubbing Hedberg over the head with a spiked bat. I could feel the swing, two-handed over my shoulder, with the nails digging deep into his skull. It felt odd being in the relaxed glow of after sex and thinking of violence, but my male Neanderthal ancestors left me little choice.

"Nice," I repeated.

"Oh Jesus, relax," she said, sensing my tense up.

"What do you expect me to say to that?" I ask. "That is a completely irrelevant thing to blurt out, especially after I just fucked you—well, I might add."

"I'm just making a statement, Jesus Christ. You men are all the same."

I wanted to say that yes, we are all the same, and you should be fucking thankful for that, sister. If we were still clubbing ourselves to death over women, you'd be in a different world, passed around like a fancy rock.

But she couldn't know this was what I was thinking; it was that miscommunication of intent. Our vantage points were from different mountaintops. Mine was from the peak of protection, since she was who I was currently fucking. I wanted to make sure it stayed that way until I no longer wanted it that way. Her perspective was one of pure freedom. I was there and provided what was needed, so she was fucking me, *for now*. She was base jumping off of my peak, swaying in the raging chaos of youth.

"I'm sure we all are the same," I said to her, deciding to agree and end that track. I racked my brain for a derailment.

"If nothing else, I'm sure he'll remember *you* for a while." I smiled and *clinked!* my glass to hers.

She smiled back. "That's true!"

Then she laughed and sipped her wine. She leaned over and kissed me.

"Thank you for tonight."

"It was a great time," I agreed. Her having manners enough to remember to thank me lightened things a bit; it mattered. We finished our wine and curled up naked. She took her boots off before sliding up next to me beneath the sheets, and we slept up against each other; her head beneath my arm in my shoulder, protected from all of the dangers she did not even know existed, present or future, snapped safely back up to my peak by the bungee cord of youth.

Less than a month later, Mitch Hedberg, comedian extraordinaire, was declared dead. Samantha and I had become distant during this month; we still drank and fucked, but we both knew the end was coming. How it would play out remained to be seen, but it was there. She had energy and innocence and a dancer's body to offer me. I had my resources and experience that she was temporarily interested in to offer her. I had solidity, which appealed to her, but not as much as the possibility, or potential, to mold another's consistency. Felines want to play, but they want to be able to direct the play: it's their way or indifference. She would find some younger guy soon enough, so I just rode the train, paying my tickets at various stops, for as long as we attracted each other. She would be around until she realized that unlike a younger guy, she wasn't going to get me to change my ways.

In the end, this made me realize that males are much more complex creatures than females; taming us is much more difficult, and as with anything, the interest always lies within the challenge. Like magnets, we are end-on-end opposites—but put beside each other, we fit perfectly. Maintaining that magnetic field to keep things perfectly aligned is the trick, regardless of age.

Half-Mast at Fort Knox

"Boom, boom, bang, bang, lie down; you're dead." That's what the song said, and that's how I felt. I was in the Fletcher Memorial Home. Or, I would have been, had my name been Fletcher. Instead, I was in a home that hadn't earned a name. You need to be dead and remembered to be a memorial, and neither my house nor I had achieved that yet. In attempts to avoid that, or at least delay it, I filled the home with loud music and cats and left the windows open so that the sounds of traffic and airplanes could come in and try to drown the silence. But nothing could drown that silence; it was constant and methodical. Like the inaudible drip of an IV.

I might have been pacifying myself with the drink, but that's only what the psychiatrist would say. I wasn't pacifying anything; I was feeding something. A better psychiatrist would have said that. A psychologist might have even gone far enough to help me figure out what it was I was feeding. But who has the time to endure that kind of therapy? A psychiatrist is the way to go, especially if you serve as your own.

"Nobody is ever completely happy," Chevy had said earlier as we sat up on the porch. "It's the human condition. If you don't have something to eat you up, you'll find something. Then you'll fight it all the way."

We agreed to the obvious and the cliché, which the beer helped flow easily. But we talked out of one side of our mouths while feeding the other, like woodchippers spewing logs into mulch. We were starving for substance, for real answers, but couldn't find the nutrients to fill us. We let the excrement of what we digested fall right out of our mouths and patted ourselves on the back with nothing to burp up but the rum-soaked breath of what we fought all the way. Neither rich, nor dead, nor remembered, we were left to our own devices of exploration, to flail wildly through life's fool's gold.

And that's what the song said, "Lie down, you're dead. *Boom, boom, bang, bang.*" The words seemed funny but sad to me, which is how the truth always sounds.

"Gotta get home to the wife and kids," Chevy said, topping off his tallboy can, crumpling it in his hand and tossing it off of the porch and into the dumpster that took up half of the yard.

"Thanks for the smokes. We on for the rescreening of *Combustion* this weekend?"

"Yeah, we're on," I said.

After he left in his oversized SUV, I decided to ring up the rest of the usual suspects. I wouldn't mind getting out.

"I can't go out tonight, in the doghouse," said the first one I rang up.

"Can't go out tonight, work," said the second.

"No can do, baby on the way," said the third.

I'd struck out. It was me, the cats, and the IV.

I cursed the oncoming evening for what it was becoming. I cursed getting up in the morning for what it would be. I moved the ashtray, smokes, glass, and phone off of the porch and placed them at the typewriter. I went back to the screen door and latched it, placed the mini-ironing board upon it, and set the plastic bin of Christmas wrapping paper up against that and a large golden pot up against that.

Fort Knox.

I had a cat that would do anything to escape. So far, he'd chewed through screen and several layers of chicken wire and wood to get out. I had to admire his spirit, but if he made it through this contraption, I would have to get an electric collar—if the raccoons didn't chew him up first.

At the typewriter, I loaded the sheet of paper and took a drink. Then I decided to refill the drink. I made sure I had enough stock. Good to go on the rum and soda and smokes.

Back at the typewriter, the paper looked at me and said, "You'll never be remembered."

I sat back for a second, looking at it. *Did this page just taunt me?*

I said back to it, "If I fill you up with the right combination of words, words that people love or hate, even words that people fight over, I'll be remembered. Somebody famous said that once, I think."

"But they will be indifferent," the little page said back, "the words and the people who read them. You don't even have an appetite of your own. How are you going to feed something to somebody else?"

"Well, if I write, I'm feeding you. And feeding you is coming from me, right?"

I swear that blank page just smirked at me, sitting there all high and mighty and white. Loaded and empty. It fluttered a little in a breath from the ceiling fan and then said, "Right. What's that you're drinking there?"

"Rum. What of it?"

"An empty drink."

"What of it?" I asked, feeling like a broken record.

"You're feeding yourself with nothing, empty of calories, of substance—nothing in, nothing out."

"Look at you! A blank page analyzing *me*!"

I realized I was yelling at my typewriter, which was ridiculous.

"I am arguing with a goddamn piece of paper," I said aloud.

"But I could be your greatest creation," the page jested back.

"You could be kindling," I told the pulp.

"I could be a love letter or a suicide note," it said. "If you were capable of either."

"Sure, you could be the Great American Novel."

"Let's not get out of hand here." It laughed.

I ripped it out of the machine with a quick jerk. It pulled out of the roller with a *vvwwwhhip* and rolled itself a little in fear. I held it up.

"You're pretty uppity for something that's about to reduce its visible surface space by about one thousand percent."

"Oh, that's going to help," it pompously fluttered.

I rolled the piece of paper into a ball, a real tight little ball, and threw it on the floor, which shut it up real quick. The cat came out from somewhere and began batting it around.

"How you like that for a creation?" I said and loaded another piece of paper.

But I realized that asshole piece of paper was right; I'd never be remembered. It was the truth. It was funny, like smashing your knuckles into glass while breaking into your own house only to find the key above the door later was funny. It was also sad, like rescuing your pet from a raccoon only to have it attack you later in a rabid, frothy rage was sad. But that could also be funny, if it happened to somebody else.

The next page didn't speak to me, which was preferable. But neither did the keys of the typewriter; the whole contraption was dead. Or my fingers were. Did it matter? It was as quiet as my IV.
I watched the cat bat the paper around for a minute, finished a smoke, and then went to refill my drink. The faucet dripped, slow and methodical, like everything else, but somehow still louder than the cars below and airplanes flying overhead.
I timed my pour to three drips. There's an art to a good drink. First, you need plenty of ice. Don't worry about skimping on the ice to get more liquid in the glass unless you're at a bar. In a bar, it's perfectly acceptable to complain about too much ice. At home, load up on the ice. Next, pour a touch of your mixer in first and then no less than three fingers of booze, no matter what size of glass. I'd suggest four or five for a tumbler or juice glass if you aren't a professional. Then top it back off with your mixer. The object is to surround your subject with distractions.

While pouring in the kitchen, I heard a *crash*!
I knew immediately what it was. The goddamn cat had knocked over the container and the ironing board and was no doubt already through the screen. I didn't stop what I was doing; at least one of us was getting out tonight. So much for Fort Knox.

While stirring my fresh drink—you must stir—I looked through the small kitchen window down at my neighbor's yard. A chaise lounge was set out where the beautiful wife sunned herself. A hose was half coiled where they bathed the dog. A grill was at the side of the garage where the husband cooked July 4 burgers and corn on the cob. I'd watched that wife many drunken afternoons, sunning in her bathing suit, tan, living the American Dream—the trophy wife. I'd masturbated to the American Dream. *Boom, boom, bang, bang.* We all have. In silence and unremembered, we all have.

We might as well lie down and be dead, pretending we're all a Fletcher, worthy of a memorial. Then maybe, just once, there wouldn't be a morning to curse. There'd be no dreams left to fight, and we could eat mulch until we burst like firecrackers.

The Dharma Arsonist

There are three people in Lou's besides me this early on Easter Sunday. I'm having a beer and watching golf on the thirteen-inch TV mounted above the bar. You have to be pretty far gone to be in a bar at this time of day, on this particular day. But I'm enjoying just sitting here with my beer and golf and Jeanne's ass. Jeanne is the bartender, who's bouncing up and down the length of the bar, cleaning this, shelving that. I'm watching this show when Chevy seats himself at the bar next to me.

"Two Bloody Marys," he says to Jeanne.

His usual smirk sticks out from below his baseball cap and sunglasses, but there is a subtle difference about him today. I look him up and down; the usual cloud of smoke issues from a cigarette butt in his fingers, hanging around him like the veil of dirt around Pig-Pen from the Charlie Brown comics. His shorts are cutoff khakis and ratty at the edges; his shirt is just as torn. There is nothing overtly different that I can spot; he is as unkempt as usual.

The drinks arrive before us, and before I can even take the straw out of mine, Chevy has downed half of his. He sits back and wipes his mouth, sighing contentedly.

"You remember Roberta Bennett?" he asks me.

"Sure. Brunette. The crazy one. Been a long time since I heard that name."

I inspect him again. Is it new shoes? A winning lottery ticket? What makes a man appear so...unburdened?

"Right," he says.

"Sure, I remember her."

"I burned her house down last night," he says with the slightest satisfied smile on his lips.

"What?"

"I was trying to spell her name in the lawn with gasoline, like in that movie. It just got a little out of control. Burnt the shit right to the ground, I'm pretty sure."

I look over his shoulder expecting to see the cops come bursting in to crack him one on the head and take him away, but the only thing coming through the door is a breeze that smells like Easter perfume and eggs Benedict. The breakfast place next door must be crowded with after-church families. The odor of sweets and food nearly turns my stomach.

"But you haven't seen that crazy bitch for five years."

"I thought it would be a nice gesture. Y'know, romantic. After such a long time, you need to do something big. Something to say, 'Hey, I've really been thinking about you.'"

"That *is* kind of romantic," I agree.

"Well, it probably would have been, except she went and got married."

"Whoops," I say. "So how'd that go over?"

"I got chased down the street by her man, who was waving a shotgun at me, completely naked," he says.

"Wait. You were naked when you fried her lawn with gasoline?"

"No, *he* was naked. For a second, I thought he might catch me, but then I just turned on the juice. I knew he couldn't hit me with those pellets once I got a good block ahead, all zigzagging and shit."

"So they got a good look at you?"

"Sure they did. I stood there grinning like a retard when she came to the door, all proud and shit, until I realized the fire was creeping a little closer to the house than I'd thought it would. Then her man showed up with the gun, and I just ran." He sticks his hand out in front of him when he says this. "Ran for a full mile before I realized he wasn't chasing me anymore. Thought I was going to lose a lung."

"You are definitely a retard," I say.

"Maybe," he says.

Jeanne comes up to refill our drinks and gives Chevy a shake of the head; she's obviously been listening in on our conversation.

"Don't be bringing any trouble in here with you. I don't need it today. I'm closing up at two; gotta see my son and his bastard father for Easter dinner."

As she says this, I get a brief whiff of pancakes from next door as someone enters the bar, letting in unwelcome sunlight and the scent of syrup. I finish my drink off quickly before it starts to taste like a short stack.

"I'm opening back up at six," Jeanne continues, "bring all the trouble you want then. I'll probably welcome it."

She leaves the drinks in front of us and sashays away, *boing, boing, boing*. I can't take my eyes off of that ass, until I see at the far end of the bar, Linda has taken a seat. Jeanne begins pouring her one.

"Hey, Linda just came in." I nod to Chevy. She is out of earshot, so we both look over, and she raises her glass a few inches to us.

"All dressed up like she just came from church even," he says.

"I have to admit, she looks pretty good. Why haven't either of us hit that?"

"Because she's a nut job," Chevy matter-of-facts. "Neither of us needs that kind of headache."

"I don't know what's worse: fucking a nut job or keeping company with a pyromaniac retard."

"Hit it then, and you'll find out."

"Maybe I will." I think about it for a moment. "I've got nothing else to do today."

"You got it all figured out, man," Chevy says, downing half of his next drink in one gulp.

At about one thirty, I'm leaving with Linda, and Jeanne is getting ready to close up. Chevy is putting the moves on Jeanne, but she looks like she's having none of it.

"What? I should invite you over so you can try to burn my place down too?" she yells at him.

"It was a beautiful fire," he tells her.

Linda and I push through the door and walk out into the blinding daylight. I have to shield my eyes. We walk between a couple of minivans parked on the street, past a couple of kids in suits and dresses, and two blocks over to my apartment. It's an old converted house, termite eaten and falling apart in places, but it maintains a quaint feel. In the kitchen, Linda is already being flirty; she's standing behind me with her hand down my pants as I pour us drinks. The cats scamper about as we toast to Easter and then start making out. We take it into the bedroom.

It's a nice, slow fuck. The kind made for Sunday afternoons. She wants it from behind, so I give it to her, but at a snail's rhythm, forward and back. Through the window, the sun is still blinding, but it looks good on her pale cheeks in my hands, *boing, boing, boing.* The whole world is caught in a nice, slow fuck.

I finish on the small of her back and grab the kitchen towel, my fading hard-on flapping up and down with a *boing* of its own. She waits patiently with her head in the pillow for me to clean it up. Then we both lay there on our backs, staring up at the ceiling where the branches play in the light and little silhouettes of birds flit about. It's peaceful. It's Easter Sunday; why shouldn't it be?

"Did he really burn somebody's house down?" Linda asks. Her hands are folded on her stomach, and her chest heaves up and down with her breathing.

"I have little doubt that he did," I say.

"I hope nobody got hurt," she blurts. I am trying to relax, but now instead I have to think of that crazy bitch Roberta going up like a match and her naked man flapping around with a shotgun like some screaming ape.

"Why'd you have to say that?"

"Why wouldn't I wonder that?"

We lay there for a minute. Maybe she did get hurt, I think. Then I think, so what if she did? Then I think that it was interesting that I didn't even think to *think* whether she was hurt in the first place. Did I not care, or was I so detached that I didn't even bother to *think to care*? The silhouettes of the branches on the ceiling lap like flames now as I stare up, wondering this.

"Goddammit," I say. "How am I supposed to relax now?"

I get up to grab my drink, flaccid and desensitized. I'm already counting the hours until Jeanne opens back up. Does the nightmare begin at home, or does it begin outside and let itself in? In this case, I blame the outside. I was perfectly happy before concern fell out of Linda's mouth like a chewed glob of those sickly sweet pancakes.

I begin to get dressed. Linda joins me, and there is that awkward air where one assumes she has said something stupid to fuck up, and in this case, she's right.

"I'm sorry," she says.

"For what?" I say, not really wanting to have a conversation. Golf is on TV, or maybe I want to write a little, I'm not sure.

"It's just what popped in my head. I just hoped everyone was all right."

"Saying what pops in your head is your gender's fatal flaw," I say, taking my drink into the next room and flipping on the TV.

In a minute, she walks in, dolled all back up with her shoulders hunched and her handbag in her hand. Her hair is matted and slightly sweaty on one side from the pillow. Still, she's a decent-looking woman. I decide not to tell her about the hair.

"I guess I'll just go," she says in that half-dejected way some women have of not really asking a question but expecting an answer anyway. Well, I wasn't going to answer an unasked question. Maybe the hair was just an extra ploy for sympathy.

"All right, bye," I say. Decent-looking or not, I am not about to ask her to stay.

She stands there for a second and then says, "You're such an asshole," as she turns and slinks out.

There is golf on the TV; he is making another late charge for a win. *Birdie, birdie, birdie.* The guy is amazing: pure grace under pressure. A true champion. Champions probably know how to answer the unasked questions without looking like assholes. I guess that's what separates him and me, and I drink to it. I've got nothing else to do today.

At six, I walk back over to Lou's. Jeanne's already opened up, and Chevy is there, still looking loose and unburdened and unkempt. There is a line of glasses in front of him as if he'd never left.

"Jeanne let you stay?" I ask, sitting next to him. I nod to Jeanne for a beer.

"So how was it?" he asks, ignoring my question, which was apparently an answer.

I think about his question for a moment. "I'm glad to have a pyromaniac retard for a friend," I concede to him.

"I won't say I told you so," he lies.

Jeanne walks over and dust-rags the area in front of us. She flashes a pretty smile at Chevy for a second and replaces his ashtray with a fresh one.

"How was the broken family dinner?" I ask her as she walks away.

She shoots me a head shake, and the smile fades. I knew it was a bad question before I even asked it, so why did I ask it?

"Fucking nightmare," she says and walks away. She moves slower, and this time as I watch, her ass goes *thump, thump, thump*.

I scan the bar; we are the only ones in the joint. Nobody else is a lost cause enough to have come back for Easter evening cocktails. It is getting dark outside, and a breeze is picking up; thankfully, the breeze is free of syrup and perfume. The church families are home, counting their eggs. The birds are asleep in their branches. Linda is probably lighting a candle at some church praying for Roberta to regrow her imaginary burnt head of hair.

And here I am, with Jeanne and Chevy and a dead jukebox.

And I realize that I don't care, and along with that, I am finally able to grasp the subtle difference in Chevy today: the looseness, the lack of burden.

"It's better to be the one starting a fire than the one jumping into one," I say to him.

"You got it all figured out, man," he says, downing the rest of his drink in one gulp.

Retard or not, Chevy is a champion.

Bravissimo

It all starts on the drive back from Daytona.

"Why aren't we married?" Cathy asks, and I know right away this is trouble.

"You're just saying that because we just came from a wedding," I say.

It's not what I'm really thinking; I'm thinking about math. I've got Tums in the bathroom cabinet and thirty miles left to go. At seventy miles an hour, that's going to take me how long to get to them?

"No, I'm not saying it because of the goddamn wedding," Cathy insists.

I turn down the music. We ride in silence for a few miles. The flat, boring expanse of I-4 westbound crawls by. The interstate practically shoots north-south, so the even number betrays its true direction. It makes me wish I had a car like Jason's, one of those Italian jobs with a name that ends in the letter "*i*" and looks like a speedy little red rat.

"Look, it's perfectly natural for this to come up after watching someone else get hitched. But we've talked about this."

"You mean, I've talked about it, and you've listened," she says.

I sigh but keep it mostly to myself. The conversation is already so cliché it's giving me a headache on top of this lurking case of heartburn. To give her the satisfaction of a full sigh might egg on the headache more.

"Are there any Tums in the glove box? Or aspirin?" I ask.

"Is that all you have to say to this? You need a fucking Tums?" she yells.

"Check the goddamn box!"

She yanks open the glove box, roots around, and then slams it shut.

"No Tums, you'll have to manage."

I'm having trouble drawing breath, but it happens; it'll pass. It was the onions in those little pizza bites at the reception, I just know it. I kick up the speedometer to eighty.

"Are you going to answer me?" she asks.

"Aren't you happy with how things are with us?"

She takes a minute to formulate a response. As a man, I know this is not good. It's better to have women flying off the handle and saying completely irrational things. When they formulate though, you've got problems.

"Happy? I don't know," she finally says.

"So this isn't something new?"

"I don't know," she repeats. Rather than call her out on the hypocrisy of her demanding an answer from me and then giving me that flaky garbage, I let it slide.

We're getting closer to home. Lake Mary passes, Longwood, Altamonte Springs. I figure I should try to resolve this before we pull in the driveway so we can have tipsy sex and watch sitcom repeats in bed until we fall asleep. But with her attitude and my aching head and constricted airways, I just can't figure an angle. I'm at eighty-five right now. If we get pulled over, I might still have enough booze in my system from the wedding reception to get the cuffs.

I decide to offer a truce. "Listen, why don't we have a nice, romantic dinner tomorrow night? We'll hit Bravissimo's and then walk down to the park." I can see Orlando rising before us now. The sign reads "Downtown: Next 4 Exits." The home stretch.

After some formulation, she says, "Okay. But slow down." It seems I've dodged a bullet. Traffic is light. The streets are empty, as most people are settling in for the night, laying out their shirts for work, tying up the garbage, dreading the beginning of another week of ridiculous bread-earning. I make it home in good time, race upstairs, and pop a few Tums and a BC Powder in the bathroom. After that, Cathy and I lie in bed and watch *MASH* until we fall asleep. We don't say much, but everything seems all right. I'm able to breathe, and the pounding in my head has subsided.

The next day, I get up and get ready for the job. Who the hell has a Sunday wedding anyway? People can't let loose at the reception because they have to work the next day. It's just an all-around bad idea—kind of like how taking your girlfriend, who is prone to grandiose romanticism, to a wedding is.

I drive in, get a shitty parking space, and settle in to my desk. Coffee, e-mail, and inane conversation get my day started right.

"So how was the wedding?" asks Jason, my co-worker with the fancy car. He also has a coke problem, but it doesn't matter to me. It's nice to know who to call if I ever decide I'm sleeping too much.

"It was all right."

"Nail any hot bridesmaids?"

"If you can imagine the opposite of that, it might sum it up."

"Ouch," he says.

And that's exactly how my next eight hours feel.

Traffic on the way home is backed up. I-4 eastbound, or should I say, northbound, is congested from constant construction. I'm in the wrong racket; I should be in a labor union for roads in this state. Those guys must make a killing. It's forty-five or less all the way; the lost tourists and local idiots change lanes without reason, hit their brakes without reason—driving without reason, as far as I know. The traffic all seems aimless.

Pulling in the driveway, I wind up feeling I need an aspirin again. I pop the BC, change into some jeans and a T-shirt, grab a beer, and flip on ESPN.

The phone jingles, but I let it ring. My legs are comfortable on the coffee table. After eight hours of answering phones, nothing could be more important than my beer and stories of athletes too stupid to stay off of steroids or coke. I have no problem admitting that I enjoy watching some asshole piss away a multimillion-dollar career because he's weak, just like the rest of us. Do ex-athletes become Italian car salesmen? I wonder.

After five rings, Cathy says, "Hey, hon, it's me," into the answering machine. "A few of us from work decided to go have some wine. Bad day at the office. We're going to Bravissimo's, so I'll already be there. Meet me."

I can show up when I want to now. Her officemates were nothing special; they bored the piss out of me. So I let ESPN drone pleasantly along with my beers. After that, a commercial makes me kind of horny, so I go into the bathroom to knock one out, and in my head, I defile three bridesmaids.

At around eight o'clock, I start to get a little hungry, so I put the shoes back on and walk down to the restaurant. It's a nice night out, maybe a little humid, but the mosquitoes aren't bad at all.

At the bar, I order a glass of Shiraz; I'm too full of beer to keep on with that. I look around for Cathy and her annoying co-workers' table. I find the table out on the patio in the smoking section. It's a decent enough atmosphere out here with little netted snifter-shaped candleholders, checkered tablecloths, and potted plants everywhere.

She is with another couple; I take the open chair next to some frumpy, middle-aged woman. I haven't met these two before. Introductions go around. The frumpy woman is Sarah; her boyfriend is Sam. I shake hands and launch into the obligatory chitchat:

"So, Sam, what do you do in the office?"

"I'm in accounting," he says.

"Oh," I say, already bored. "That's interesting."

"Not really," he says, and I kind of like Sam all of a sudden.

It turns out that Sarah works in the same department as Cathy. It becomes the shoptalk channel, Cathy and Sarah prattling about office romance this, jerkoff boss that, waste of resources this. Sam and I just kind of sip our wine and nod. I can tell Sam is paying attention out of obligation—probably less to Sarah than to some sort of imagined work duty. That's the problem with drinking with co-workers. What the fuck else do you really have in common besides work? I feign interest as well, for Cathy's sake.

"So," Sarah wraps up an unnecessarily long story, "that's what I told him. You...can't...have...it...both...ways." The girls laugh; Sam grins. I time my sip right so I don't have to sham a response. It's some kind of punch line to some inside joke, I figure. Why would I find it funny?

The waitress shows up and deters the beginning of another story. We order our meals. I decide I'm going to tip her extra well for her timing. Plus, she's really exotic-looking, a rare beauty. After she trots off, Sarah starts another story anyway, like she had them queued up on cards in her frumpy cleavage.

If I couldn't be a labor union rep for transportation, I'd like to be a beauty like that waitress. There are plenty of ways to make killings in this world. Hell, maybe I'd marry an athlete.

The rest of the meal goes similarly. Afterward, we all walk outside, and good-byes are said to Sarah and Sam. Sam and I shake, and we share that nod, the nod of the bored boyfriend. It's an unspoken bond.

Sarah gives me the friendly hug. "Nice to finally meet you; Cathy's said so much about you." Underneath her dress, she feels like a sack of potatoes. They pull off, and Cathy and I watch them go while holding hands.

"Up for that walk?" I ask, somewhat hoping she says no.
"Sure."

So we walk. We head down Shine to Central, hang a left into the park. The park is small, but done up well. We live in a historic neighborhood. The trees in the park grow every which way and hang themselves just over your head; there are a few benches and old-time gas-style street lamps. We're the only people there. We find a bench and sit.

"So, Sam seems like a pretty laid-back guy," I say.

"Good choice of words. He's getting laid off next week. He doesn't know yet."

"That's too bad," I say, thinking it's probably the only honest thing I've said all day—or the second. I was honest to Jason.

"He's a nice enough guy," Cathy agrees.

"What's up with him and Sarah?" I ask in a confused tone.

"Meaning what?"

"Meaning Sarah looks like she should be home feeding her five cats and knitting in a rocking chair."

"Sarah's not a spinster. And she's my friend, you ass."

"All right, okay. They just seem like a mismatched couple."

"Hmm," Cathy says under her breath.

"This is kind of romantic here," I say, looking around, figuring it must be and hoping the subject change will work. Perhaps bringing up Sam and Sarah was too close to home for Cathy and me.

"If you say so," she says.

We sit there some more, as if what to do next will be revealed to us. Instead, we just wind up sitting there some more. My heartburn starts to kick in again, and I can only think, *What the fuck?* Onion in the sauce, I realize. *Dammit.* I am starting to develop into an old man. Next, it will be Metamucil and blood-pressure pills. It leads to thoughts of old age. Will I be alone? Would I be passing up something good with Cathy if we broke up right here, right now? I don't know. I feel like I-4, all congested and running contrary to things.

"Do you think Sam and Sarah will make it?" I ask.

"She's dumping him when he gets fired," Cathy says.

"Poor guy," I say.

"Yeah," she says, "poor guy."

"Well, at least we don't have to worry about that," I say, not really sure at all what that means.

Cathy sits there, formulating, I realize. Is she formulating marriage and knitting and cats and rocking chairs? I have no idea; I'm a man.

"Yeah, we have each other," she says.

It makes me feel like I just dodged a bullet. It makes me feel like I just took a bullet. I stare off into the distance at the skyscrapers, through those low-hanging trees. I don't feel like going to work tomorrow.

"I wonder what episode of *MASH* is on tonight," I say, putting my arm around Cathy. She shuffles closer to me on the bench and settles her head into my shoulder. An animal of some kind makes a sound across the park—maybe it's lonely, maybe just saying hello for no reason.

"It doesn't matter; they're all good," she says into my shoulder, but I'm already thinking about math. I've got Tums in the bathroom cabinet. It's half a mile back to the house...How fast does a couple walk?

Vintage Chevy

We'd finally been kicked out of Lou's Lounge one too many times, so we found ourselves drinking at a Houlihan's restaurant on a Tuesday. Houlihan's is one of those semi-upper-end franchise deals with the smoking patio that has J. Geils Band pumping out of the wall speaker. They know their demographic, and Chevy and I are not a part of it. The thin metal chairs hurt my ass, and the imitation sandstone tables and modern glasses hip the place up, so they charge more for drinks. All those things really do, in Florida, is cause condensation to fall off of the glass and make a mess everywhere. So I shuffle my ass cheeks around a lot and ask for extra napkins every few minutes.

"They *do* have better-looking waitresses," Chevy says, as some nubile nineteen-year-old drops off our Captains. We both watch her skip back inside to the bar.

"Than Lou's? That's not a stretch." Lou's didn't even have waitresses.

"No, but all of these near-twenties hotties in the slinky black outfits might make the overpriced drinks worth it."

Without any waitresses around to look at, we survey the patio. There is a table of late-thirty-something women to the side of us, two spots down. More concerned with pounding our rum and Cokes, we choose not to talk to them. But several vultures have begun to form a circle around them; the forty-something divorcees smell drunk meat.

We watch the table for a short while. They're doing the *Glory Days* routine; stories of college go around. You have your typical ex-frat washout with his quieter friend who probably got beat up by guys like him back in the day, but now makes more money, so Frat Washout clings on to the tail of his slick sports coat. Then you have Banker Bob. Rail thin with a head of thick, white hair, Bob is a functional alcoholic and a very sharp dresser who is a staple here at Houli's. Bob is also blessed with the gift of gab; give him three seconds, and he'll monopolize your entire evening.

Seated, you have the drunk meat: the ex-sorority sister, the obligatory mousy one who just gives eyes, and then the too-tipsy one who keeps catching herself before spilling what a slut she was back in college.

"I know! I know! We'd have these great parties after the games," she'd say. "This one time in my friend's dorm room, we were partying with a few guys and someone brought out a dildo…"

There would be a bit of silence as she thrust her drink into her mouth to shut it up.

One of the other women would then pipe in some inane question to the men, like, "Did you play any sports?"

The men would fumble over themselves to rattle off what they did.

Bob, however, just listens.

I am saddened to see the demographic that might be me, sooner rather than later—partly because I didn't go to a college that had any sports at all; my string of failing out of community colleges wouldn't compete. I'd never get laid in a situation like this—even with these harpies. And I hoped I'd never have to try; I'd rather drink myself into a vomiting stupor than play this game. Not that I didn't do that as it was already. Drink myself into stupors, that is.

"See what we've been missing by going to dive bars, Chevy?" I say to him, just out of earshot of the vultures and drunk meat.

"Fuck it," he says. "It's your fault we're here anyway."

"Exactly. It was my punch that broke Jeanne's nose, you errant-ass motherfucker," I remind him of his last heroic act at Lou's.

Chevy has a hidden angry streak that comes out sometimes when he drinks. Not that that is unusual—he just has horribly unfortunate aim with his fists. His last attempt at a swing had missed the drunken idiot he was trying to hit and instead gave our bartender a bloody nose. The straw that broke Lou's Lounge's back.

"Whatever." He shrugs it off. "You in a gambling mood tonight?"

"I'm always in a gambling mood."

"The table there, it's interesting." He nods toward the middle-aged dating game a few tables away. "I bet I can predict who gets laid. Loser pays the tab."

"Say what?"

"You have three on three there. Who's gonna score with who?" His eyes light up at the thought of wagering on it.

"Unless it's me with that slinky nineteen-year-old in there..." I point at the bar door. "...it doesn't make a damn bit of difference to me."

"Nah," he says, "I mean, do you think Bob can hold his own with these guys?"

I twist my head to look back over at the table where the birds of prey are still circling the carrion. Banker Bob does look sharp. The other two schmucks are prototypical—tucked-in button-downs with chest hair showing and cocky—vultures wishing they were roosters, just bobbing their heads along and fluffing feathers at each other with no real henhouse to claim, waiting for the prey to die or at least be immobilized before picking at the eyes.

"I don't know; those guys might have twenty years on Bob," I tell Chevy.

"Persistence," he says. "He's got the years to tough out the long ones. You can't trust his slurring; it's a ploy."

"So you say Bob scores first?"

"Hell no! I bet he takes them *all* home, and those hyenas standing there go home empty-handed."

"I see them more as vultures. Definitely cowardly, like scared, starving birds."

"Hyenas, vultures, what's the difference? They're both scavengers."

"You've got a point, but Bob taking all three? That's a tall bet. You dying to lose?"

"I'll gamble any odds anytime." He holds out his hand to shake on it. I take it.

"Done," I say, hoping he actually winds up winning this one despite the fact that this tab was likely to near triple digits at this ridiculous franchise bar with its ridiculous wildlife.

Our firm little waitress refills us, and we go back to discussing our press idea, work or lack thereof, and other things. The buzz is kicking in nicely tonight, and there's not a lot of humidity. It helps keep the head clear so that it doesn't get weighed down with the alcohol and all that water-filled air that makes it so hard to breathe and drink. The only problem so far tonight is my sore left ass, but there's little to be done about that, I figure, except switch over to the right. The sun has fully set, but the mosquitoes are light, and on the wall speaker, J. Geils has been replaced by the Go-Go's.

"My band used to cover this song," I say, as I pull the lime from my drink and throw it on the table where it rests with a pile of other limes in a bath of pooled condensation. I've told our young wonder of nature in black three times, "*No lime*," and every time, there's lime. I guess when you're a beautiful infant on top of the world, you don't need to be on top of the small things, like your tip.

"'Vacation.' Good song," Chevy says, taking a healthy drink.

"Yeah, we punked it up and shit. Then this band named Mu330 stole it after we opened up for them."

Chevy just nods. He hates punk and probably has no idea what a Mu330 is. He sets his drink down, getting back on the publishing topic. "So, we get the ISBNs, incorporate, and set up printing with Doubleday. Fidlar, whatever."

"Which is only about five hundred out of pocket," I say.

"We gotta print some real shit. No pussy shit. I want writing that tears the ass out of the reader—gritty, real."

"Transgressive. No pussy shit," I say. "We're looking at about another four or five hundred a run, maybe six. Limited, with shared marketing push."

"All right."

"I already got a site in the works."

"And Rommel has the legal side covered."

"All that shit," I say.

"Good. No pussy shit though."

"Not unless it's our own."

"Oh shit, check it out," Chevy says, as his eyebrows shoot up and he nods at something behind me.

I look back over at the roadkill table. Bob is making his play.

"These are my two daughters," he's telling the gaggle of over-the-hill women. He's got his wallet open and is leaning over the table, completely cutting off the other two men. It's working on the women; they're gushing, "Oh, they're *sooo* cute!" The vultures look disoriented. Something alive has strayed into their circle.

"They're my little flowers," Bob says. "Of course, they don't live with me. But I love 'em both." Bob puts his hand to his chest as he says this to drive his point home, and the three women say *"Awwww"* in unison.

I turn back to Chevy for a second to tell him that "goddamn, Bob is a smooth cat."

"So why do they call you Banker Bob?" the sorority sister asks. You'd never know she used to be a cheerleader; she's a lumpy sack of sag with a huge perm and thighs so fat they could suffocate her son's soccer coach.

Bob half turns and points his finger toward the sky. "You see that building over there?"

"The bank building, yeah."

"Well, that's where I work."

"Ohhh!" the gaggle says in unison.

"I'm the parking attendant in the garage."

For some reason, the gaggle finds this funny, and they all laugh. I realize that if they are laughing at that kind of shit already, Bob is *in*. I'm not the only one to notice it; the hyenas take a step back and start talking about football loudly, trying to play off the fact that Bob has just outplayed them.

"Damn, looks like you're getting close to winning your drink," I tell Chevy.

"I already have; you'll see," he says to me smugly.

"Not yet. Bob has to take his pick; there is still a one-to-one ratio."

"No, you're missing it. They're pussy shits," he says.

"Huh?"

"They're pussy shits; they've already given up—the hyenas. Bob doesn't have to pick. Bob's goin' beyond the ménage tonight! *Pussy shits!*" he yells.

I look over toward them, and as I do, the would-be roosters look over at us. Shit, this buzz is getting on pretty good. *Did they hear us?*

"Looks about right," I say. "Might want to tone the voice down. I bet they actually call the cops at a place like this if there's a fight. If we get kicked out of this joint, we'll be stuck drinking at the goddamn burrito stand."

"*Pussy shiiiiits!*" Chevy says loudly, with his arms outstretched, though he's looking at nobody in particular.

The entire roadkill scene looks our way. Banker Bob recognizes us.

"Hey, boys, good to see you. Got a little problem over there?" he asks, making it sound unassuming, but I am positive it is accusing.

I'm still trying to figure out how he pulled that off when Chevy replies, "Hey, Bob. We're good. How about you?"

"Excellent, excellent. Couldn't be better, son."

I raise my glass. Bob nods and smiles, and we all toast—all of us except for the vultures, and I realize that Bob has just diplomatically told us to keep it down and even managed to get a toast out of it. The ladies pay rapt attention to him as he goes on about how he lost the house and the car in the divorce, but still, his wife is a good woman and cares well for the kids. I turn back around, feeling a burning in my pocket where Chevy's half of the tab is.

"Pussy shits," Chevy snorts into his drink.

Our waitress is named Maria, we find out. Chevy is trying to set me up with her. I'm more interested in my drink. Not that she isn't cute—I'm just an alcoholic.

"He used to play in bands, you know," he says to her as she delivers our fifth or sixth round. I have lost count.

She doesn't bite, not an iota of interest.

"That band, Em-you-three stole a song from him," he says. He does not have a clue what he's talking about, but he doesn't care.

"Really," she says, picking up the pile of limes from the center of the table.

"Yeah. Go-Go's. Right?" he looks over at me. He knows damn well I am not any more interested in talking about it than she is hearing about it.

"Something like that," I say. The waitress and I grin at each other. *"Sorry"* mine says.

"Damn right you are; I'm busy," hers says.

"Fresh round in ten minutes?" she says to neither of us, looking off into the parking lot.

"Yeah," we both exhale simultaneously. I add napkins to the order. Sometimes, drinking is a chore, but it's not a duty you decline. There is something of a resigned honor in accepting that you know your next move is not a wise one, but you are going to make that move anyway.

Maria slips back into the bar. I look back over to the drunk meat, and Bob is seated at the table with them, which is good for him. Frat Washout and Successful Sportscoat Guy are staring us down, which is bad for us. They can probably take us even though we have them by a few years. They look like they work out, and we are way too boozed up and out of shape from hard drinking and general malnutrition. We had a lifetime of hard labor on our side, but even those muscles go soft sitting in front of a computer at office jobs all day.

"Look at these d-bags," Chevy says. It's not loud enough for them to hear, but reading his lips wouldn't be that difficult.

"What's up, guys?" Chevy says to them, a little louder now, offering a smile that isn't really a smile.

He is drunk already. I set down my rum and slyly palm my lighter off of the table—not that it would keep me from breaking my knuckles; I'd just always been taught to hold a lighter in your fist before dotting somebody in the eye.

"You guys got a problem?" says the over-the-hill frat guy.

I shake my head and wave them off. Though part of me wouldn't mind a fight so much, it's been a long time.

"Why would you ask that?" Chevy asks, turning their antagonism around. "You heard Bob; we're just having a drink here, fellas." When Chevy says *'fellas,'* one eyebrow rises and his mouth goes into a one-sided grin.

"You calling us gay?" says Frat Guy.

"If you two keep looking over here, there's going to be trouble."

Sportscoat puts a hand on his friend's shoulder. "Let's go inside," he says.

Suddenly, I hear the scrape of a metal chair behind me. I grip the lighter and flex my arm. I begin to turn and then finally realize it is Bob several tables away.

"*Hey*! Guys, guys! This is a family place!" he injects, the slurred voice of reason. "Now, if you need to arm wrestle or something, take it off the patio. Go on!" He makes a swooping arm motion to usher us into the lot, almost falling out of his chair as he does so. The mousy one grabs him and helps him right himself. "Thank you, darlin'," he says to her.

"We're just trying to have a drink here, Bob. How are you doing over there?" Chevy says.

"Excellent son, excellent," he says, raising his drink, and again, Bob has made his point. And again, Chevy has managed to have the exact same conversation with him. I begin to feel like this was all planned, right down to Bob getting the mousy one to help him out.

The hyenas move past us and take the door into the bar. I put my lighter back on the table. Chevy laughs, and behind me, Bob laughs with him.

I look at both of them. "What's this? A tag team?" I ask Chevy.

"Well, boys, you ought to be careful. I think I'm going to head home. Ladies?" Bob says to his table.

All four of them get up. The sagging, lumpy women shoulder their purses, push in their chairs, and walk out into the parking lot with Banker Bob.

"No fucking way," I say.

"I'll take a double," Chevy says.

Maria brings the next round out. This time, there's no lime.

"He's a writer," Chevy says, nodding toward me, refusing to give up the charade.

"That's nice," Maria says. "I thought he played in bands."

"He did," he says to her.

I am beginning to wonder if I am even sitting at this table.

"What do you write?" she asks me.

"Not a whole hell of a lot," I truthfully reply.

"Hmm."

"He's just modest; he writes for *Rolling Stone*," Chevy says.

"Hmm," Maria says.

"Hey, listen," Chevy continues, "we want to buy drinks for these two guys who were out here a few minutes ago. Button-down shirts tucked in all nice and fancy, tight jeans with actual belt buckles and shit. Know who I mean?"

"I know who you mean."

"Get them some Shirley Temples." Chevy laughs.

Maria says nothing; she just stands there.

"Ahhh." Chevy straightens up. "Get them whatever fruity thing they're drinking."

"All right," Maria says and disappears inside.

"*We* want to buy them some drinks?" I give Chevy my best you're-a-jackass look.

"Why not?" he asks.

"For starters, it's now on *my* tab, thanks to your Good Lush/Bad Lush routine with Bob there. And, on a side note, what the fuck is up with the *Rolling Stone* thing? Do nineteen-year-olds even read that magazine these days?"

"Hey, man, just trying to help you out with that." Chevy nods toward the door to show he means Maria. The issue of my tab is apparently a nonissue.

"I appreciate it," I lie. "You better worry about yourself if Jockstrap and GQ come back out."

"Man, you worry too much."

"With your aim, I can't worry enough."

We both drink for a minute. I contemplate palming my lighter again; if it comes to blows, Chevy might wind up punching himself by accident.

"So, how many books a year we going to put out?" he breaks the silence with a subject dropped twenty minutes ago. "Jessie's Girl" by Rick Springfield kicks on from the wall speakers.

"Figure from three to five books a year. One will have to be an anthology. It'll double as a contest to get traffic. Hopefully, it'll attract good writers."

"None of that poetry nonsense, I don't like that. Poetry is pussy shit."

"Only the flowery or cut-your-wrists kind," I say.

"You mean the kind you write?" he jokes.

Then, from behind us, a voice says sternly, "You like that term *pussy shit,* don't you?"

We both look up. The button-down crew came out for a smoke, and we hadn't noticed. I look on the table for the lighter and then realize I'd already grabbed it to light a smoke, which is in my better swinging hand. I switch them quickly but nonchalantly.

"What's up, guys?" asks Chevy, smiling again. They both stand at the table, holding drinks, lighting a smoke. I sit there, waiting for the first sign of a move.

"Thanks for the drink," says Sports Coat, the assumedly richer one. His shirt is nicer.

I raise mine up a little bit in toast, just as I'd done with Bob earlier.

"Tough luck with those hags over there," Chevy says, raising his drink as well.

"We're not worried about it," says Washout.

We all chuckle and do a pseudo-toast into the clear evening air.

"Nah, why would you be worried?" Chevy asks rhetorically, but I know him well enough to know that is a very subtle jab. "Wanna sit down?"

They say, "All right," and sit down. It's not as awkward as it should be. Vintage Chevy—turning things on a dime, again. I excuse myself to take a piss. I was hoping not to break the ice; now I'll be pissing all damned night.

Inside Houli's, it is mostly dead except for a few couples in the dimly lit booths. The restaurant side is practically empty, so the waiters and waitresses have all disappeared to smoke something out back. I weave through the unoccupied high tables near the televisions and duck into the men's room.

The bathroom is imitation marble—What do they use for fake marble? I suppose it is real—and wood paneled. The wood might be fake though, I surmise. I let go six rounds of rum and Coke. The place is too pristine, so I spread it around a little bit. It makes me miss the crusted shit can in Lou's. There isn't a word of graffiti in the whole area, so it is a boring piss, but at least they have hot water. Lou's wouldn't give you hot water if you had to heat it to mix formula for a dying baby. On the way back out, I spot Maria in the kitchen. I offer a grin, and I'm not sure what I get in return can also be called one.

When I get back to the table, Chevy's in full chat with the hyenas.

"So what do you guys do?" he asks.

"We own the *Orlando Tribune*," says the nice shirt.

"*No shit!*" says Chevy, sitting straight up. He has the same look in his eye as when he suggested playing the drunk meat game earlier.

"No shit," deadpans the washout.

"You guys need to review some of our books. Once we put them out."

"Are you a publisher?" snorts Frat.

"Damn straight."

"What have you put out?"

"Besides your mom?" asks Chevy, mimicking Frat's deadpan.

There's a moment of decision that either precedes a fight or a good laugh, and the table chooses the laugh. After that, the conversation continues on publishing. The talk circles around books for about half a drink. Then they excuse themselves.

"Okay, guys, thanks for the drink. It was interesting." They get up to go. GQ reaches into his sports coat and produces a card, handing it to Chevy.

"Here's my card. If you guys actually put anything out, send it directly to me. At least I know you guys are real. But if it sucks, don't expect a response."

"We don't print pussy shit," Chevy says, as if that were a response.

"We gathered that," says the washout, and they fluff their feathers and bob their heads back into the dead bar.

Not even a minute later, Maria pops outside.

"Last call," she says.

"But it's only eleven!" I say.

"Last call for you guys," she says.

"What the fuck kind of discrimination is that?" Chevy shouts, probably proving her point for her.

"Doubles then," I say. "Split tab."

"Wait a minute, I won that bet!" Chevy contends.

"No, you cheated by eliminating the competition and utilizing an outside force."

"C'mon man, that took work! Besides, don't blame me if you aren't smart enough to help your own cause."

"All right, all right, my tab," I tell her. It was worth it. Plus, ultimately, he is right.

"Yeah," Chevy says to her. "This guy here…" He nods in my direction. "…just landed guaranteed reviews in the *Orlando Tribune*."

Maria smiles at me. Or half smiles. Or forces a half smile.

"You guys be careful driving home, okay?"

"We're walking," Chevy lies. "We live right over there." He points across the parking lot.

"That's a Chick-fil-A fast-food joint." She sighs.

"That's right, baby. This guy here…" He puts his hand on my shoulder. "…just bought it."

She disappears back inside.

"That bitch is impossible to impress," Chevy says.

"See what we've been missing by going to dive bars?" I say, again.

"Hey," he replies, "if Banker Bob can nail three soccer moms and we can get an in to regional reviews, *and* you can at least look at a piece of young ass that has all of its teeth, what's wrong with that?"

"You have a point," I say, a little saddened that I've already joined the demographic, joined Banker Bob and the hyenas and the gaggle of lumpy women. Maybe it's the booze. Or the soundtrack from the wall speakers. Or the pristine bathrooms. I somehow feel twenty years older. Now I just need a few pictures of an ex-wife and a story about how she stole my children and the car and the house, and I'll have it made.

Origins of August

This stained hardwood floor used to be the color of rust and represented everything associated with rust: something worn that had given up on its shine, ignoring the suffocating buildup that served as a barrier to light and air. These walls used to gather cobwebs and close in on the bad nights until crawling inside a bottle of venom was the only way to avoid being crushed between them. The wall mural in the entrance was painted by a previous tenant—dancing, nameless, faceless people, who at one point served only as a cruel joke, forever immobile in their elated contentment. I used to sit in this cubbyhole and write out of necessity as my soul slithered from room to room attempting to escape the thoughts that chased it—necessity to get the words to the page before they ate my soul with a fervent desire for self-destruction.

The corners were blacker than my lungs and hungrier than my fears, extending far beyond their reach with tendrils that stung to the touch. The only sounds to be heard during any hour were the click and the hiss of either a bottle opening or a cigarette being lit and the tapping of fingers across keys. Words formed that only justified the past and documented the present. The moaning air conditioner easily blended in with the overbearing silence, leaving me unable to distinguish its monotonous sigh from the drone of dying humidity in absolute space. Absolute space—a setting of pitch emptiness that is the reference point in my universe to the day before you truly began.

❧❦

I gathered my soul from underneath the bed and hauled the weight of those sighs out into the world one fateful day in January. Pockets overflowing with indifference and pores sweating venom, I suited in persona and warmed up the motor of robotic ambition, watching the dust from both settle to a film that blanketed everything and clouded my eyes to the beginning of another year of sleepwalking. But fate, it turned out, had something else in store for two beings who had given up on dreaming that day, and I was one of them.

Set into the motion of learning old tricks, regaining my sea legs, I ventured outside to coat my lungs with pitch and soothe the yearning ebb of addiction in my veins.

It only took my first exhale for fate to make its play: a tornado swept in and lifted the dust into its vortex while emptying out my pockets with a vacuum draw to the sky, and as I watched the weight stream above me, I noticed something caught in the funnel. It was a blue raven with green eyes that literally sparked with everything opposite of me, and yet somehow said everything familiar to me. We met in a gaze of recognition, that split-second-yet-forever glance of two beings caught in a circumstance beyond their control with an immediate understanding that because of it, neither of them would ever be the same. I could not meet this raven's gaze for long, but you were born in that moment of spark and recognition, recognition that became a part of the whirlwind of that sudden tornado taking everything in its path with it.

☙❧

By now, you are probably familiar with Poe and might cringe at my choice of explanation for that moment, but you will also understand its necessity and why it must be as it is. For it is also why you must be as you are and why you are here. In the days since that single spark, my raven and I have been carried by a tornado that has yet to slow down and that has yet to take pity on the obstacles in its path. It levels barriers both tangible and intangible; it sometimes sucks objects into it that are too heavy to carry for long and expels them out of pure survival instinct. It sometimes just twirls in place and allows nearby residents to safely stare at it in awe. It is an entity, an entity that at its core has a serene ring of calm, and in that core lies the essence of you.

On that fateful day in January, the world of your beginning found light and air. By June, the tentacles in the corners lay severed and withered on a shiny floor and served as playthings for the cat. Music slowly started seeping from every orifice in the walls of this home that became coated with fresh paint and were decorated with pictures depicting the nucleus of the meaning of together. My lungs and heart began spotting with pink in preparation for the day that the black would be swallowed up by healthy tissue permanently—the day you chose your time to join us, the day we awaited with a new description of fervently.

As I write you this now, the walls are pulled to their limit, convex with bursting, leaving stretch marks as the dancing, nameless, faceless people frolic in the foyer and my raven and I gaze into each other's eyes for hours at a time. The floor is always the focal point where the tornado touches ground for us, our place of respite. Words form as fingers race across keys now only to glorify the present and embody hope for the future. Fear is evicted with the silence of its persona in the wake of the birth of new atoms. You are the result of the offspring of a simple spark that ignited absolute space and filled the emptiness of two sleepwalking beings. These words I write now are for you, yet only but a dream filling the rooms around us. Welcome to the meaning of together, my August.

The Downfall of Houli's

Chevy and I settle in to our temporary coffins on Houlihan's patio. Process of elimination has made this patio our haunt. The thin metal chairs are our caskets, and we fall into them willingly, despite the fact that we are sick to death of them, of it—of all of it. We're sick of the bad music from the wall speakers, the ineffective cover from the elements, and the overpriced drinks. But we have been kicked out of so many establishments that we are stuck here. Most would say we come here by choice—that there is always a choice—but as far as I'm concerned, this is all predestined. It's meant to be that we will sit here, our rum glasses creating streaks on the table, our ashes floating like fireflies that burn tiny holes in our clothes. It's meant to be that the waitresses will come out for a smoke and sit with us and chat, until they either cut Chevy or me off of liquor. Chevy and I do not care either way; each evening holds its own destiny. We're just along for the ride.

"Two double Captains," I tell Gina, who has come out to get our order. The order is rote, having been long established by now. We chat for a moment, and she shows us a new tattoo that she's gotten: a Boba Fett who stands sternly on the rest of the Star Wars ink running up her forearms. Chevy nods with approval, and Gina takes her pretty face and sizeable chest back inside.

"She gets better looking every time," he says to me.

"Still trying to get me in bed with that? What's in it for you?"

"I just want to know what it's like. I have to live vicariously through you since I'm married. So hurry up and hit it already."

"I'll see what I can do," I tell him with the least amount of commitment I can muster.

I look off of the patio and into the empty parking lot. We are on the edge of a suburban sprawl at the end of Florida winter. A streetlight goes through its color motions, alone and slightly waving in the post-winter, pre-spring breeze. The trees are curling up without their leaves, and there are no birds in them to swoop down and take food off the table. Even the drinks taste bland, thinning our tropical blood, subjecting us to the chill.

I can smell fried food from the Chick-fil-A fast-food joint across the abandoned parking lot, and looking over, I notice that an employee is leaning out of the drive-through window, staring back in our direction. So here we are; this employee and Chevy and I, with our own span of silent asphalt. Most would say by choice, but who chooses to remain alone in a gulf of concrete? Who stays back to watch the stoplights go from green to red by choice, while the rest of the world slumbers? Chevy and I are free and drinking but freezing; our companion across the lot is working but warm. How can that *not* be a destiny we have all just fluttered into, like tumbleweeds? The drive-through operator shuts the glass partition and disappears into the restaurant to be actively productive. Chevy and I take another sip of our drinks to be passively destructive.

Gina brings the drinks out and pulls up a chair. We've learned over the course of the years that she is an avid occult and sci-fi fan. She is also well read and into independent arts; it gives us all something in common.

She's brought a shot for herself, which she downs immediately and then brings her tattooed arms up to light a smoke. After we've all lit up and have leaned back in our chairs, Gina asks us what we are doing later.

"If I can still walk by the time we're done here, I'm going to be fixing that issue at home," Chevy says, instinctively taking a sip to punctuate his meaning.

"You'd better be able to walk," I tell him. "You drove here."

"Well, if you guys want to do something besides pass out, I'm going out with Maya later. She's new and hasn't been downtown, so I'm taking her to Chillers. You guys are welcome to come."

"Crowd's a bit young for me," Chevy says.

Gina looks over at me.

"I'll keep that option open."

"I've got a mountain of pills," she says, winking at me.

"In that case, I'll keep that option a little more open."

She smiles. "Fresh round?"

"Dumb question," Chevy says.

After Gina has dropped off the next round and a complimentary shot for us both, Maya, the new waitress, pops out for a cigarette. It seems Gina has filled her in on us. It makes me wonder what her description of two men sitting in their metal coffins staring off into nothing sounds like.

"You must be Chevy," she says, introducing herself with a handshake.

"Hello, Maya," I say to her, taking her small and noticeably soft hand. She's pretty—blonde hair, green eyes, petite with large breasts. I make a mental note to buy the Houlihan's hiring manager a shot someday. I like his style.

"So what do you guys do?" she asks.

"Hold these chairs down and dirty your glasses," Chevy says with only the slightest discernable sarcasm.

To her credit, she chuckles. To move things in a friendlier direction, I ask her, "So you're new here? New to Houli's, or new to Florida?"

"I just moved down here from Jersey," she says, "me and my kid. I'm staying with my grandparents for a while."

Chevy and I don't say anything for a long ten seconds as we do the math, counting the numerous red flags in her statements. Residents of this state are all running from something, and it is better not to ask for more details than you are willing to learn.

"Well, how do you like it so far?" I ask her to break the silence.

She smiles, exhaling. "Not bad! We went over to Daytona last weekend. Kyle—my kid—had never seen the beach, believe it or not. And, you know, this job isn't the greatest, but I've had much worse. Believe me."

There was no need to respond to that; we believed her.

"Anyway," she continues, "I'm looking forward to getting out with Gina tonight. I haven't been out in for*ever*!"

"Downtown is fun; you'll have a good time," Chevy says. "Hey, can you grab us two more drinks?"

Maya puts out her smoke and says, "Yep! Be right back."

Once she is inside, Chevy and I both look at each other.

"Very cute."

"Very cute. Possibly crazy."

"Possibly crazy and on the run."

"Possibly ex-stripper."

"Possibly crazy ex-husband baby daddy hunting her down."

"Possibly a real party girl. I mean, single Jersey mom at twenty? And just moved to the Sunshine State? Put the line of coke on the tip of your cock right now. It's spring break in February."

"Possibly."

"Probably."

"Yeah, probably."

And with that, we are content that we have fully dissected Maya.

She comes through the patio door with our drinks. "Here you go, guys," she says, smiling an extra second at me.

"Thanks," I say with a wry smile.

"Hey, why don't you pull up a chair for a minute, have another cigarette?" Chevy says, sliding a metal chair over to the table; it makes a screeching sound across the concrete. "We'll leave this other one open in case Gina comes out," he says. I've never understood his fascination, or maybe it was infatuation, with Gina. But he made no effort to disguise it, so I saw no fun in fucking with him about it.

Maya shrugs her shoulders and sits down next to me. She shivers, so I offer my flannel shirt; she takes it and wraps it around her petite shoulders. Though the alcohol has thinned my already sun-sheer blood, it has also started to warm me from the inside; our rum keeps the chill at bay.

"One of you got a light?" she asks. I light my Zippo and hold it up for her.

"So," Chevy says, leaning in toward the table, "we were just talking about religion. Like, whether it really matters. Or—not that, exactly—but, does it matter when it comes to…what's the word I'm looking for? Vices. Stuff like that."

"Yeah?" she says. "Religion is a touchy subject. Plus, I imagine it would matter what religion it was, wouldn't it?"

Already seeing where he is going with this, I have to nod to myself; sometimes, Chevy can be a clever motherfucker.

"Well," Chevy says, exhaling smoke, "I don't think any of it makes a fucking damn bit of difference at all. I mean, if you live a good life, you live a good life. And going to church doesn't matter. And who's to say what a good life is anyway? Am I bad because I drink and smoke? Or, if I was single, because I sleep with too many people? Who's to say? Who's to tell me? Know what I mean? That was our take on it." He winks over at me as he says this, but Maya misses it.

"My parents and grandparents would say you are a bad person." She laughs. "They're Baptist. Like, hard-core Baptist."

Chevy fakes a laugh. "Yeah! Like that, that's what I mean." He takes a gulp of his drink. "But what about you? Are you into all that? I mean—you're smoking out here with us and you work in a bar. Restaurant-bar, whatever."

Maya gets quiet for just a tick, but it's an eon of a tick, like waiting for a train to pass. I can see boxcar after boxcar roll behind her eyes in those few seconds.

"Well, I was raised Baptist, if that's what you mean. We don't believe in abortion. Sinners don't go to heaven. I believe in God and all that, and I try to live a good life. I haven't been perfect; who is? But I think it matters. It matters if you go to church and believe the Bible and not follow the godless people."

"Godless people?" I ask, genuinely curious.

"Yeah, like, scientists. Y'know, like evolution and all that. Things that go against the Bible."

Somehow, Chevy doesn't miss a beat. "Right. Like, you have to *believe*. But do you have to follow all of their *rules*?"

"Rules like what?" Maya asks Chevy.

"Oh, I don't know. Like, drinking, drugs, sex. What kinds of music they say you should listen to—stuff like that. Y'know?"

Maya laughs. "No, I guess some of religions' rules are stupid."

I know that at this second, Chevy is going to ask this girl which rules, specifically, are stupid, and this girl is going to open up like a porn star's mouth during a facial. But the patio door opens, and the bartender turtles his head through. He tells Maya to get off of her ass and take care of her tables.

"Sorry, guys, I'll be back out later," she says, handing me back my shirt.

Once she is back inside, Chevy smiles.

"Damn I'm good."

"You're good."

"She's definitely crazy. But that crazy can also be good, if it's turned bad."

"That I even *understand* what you just said worries me."

"Spring break in February."

"I might go downtown." Sex with crazy Maya was starting to sound like an enjoyable possibility.

"You'd better."

Another hour passes with Gina bringing our drinks. There's no sign of Maya. Gina tells us that it's gotten busy inside, and it is the first time in months, so they are understaffed.

I ask Gina what the deal is with Maya's whole Baptist anti-Darwin thing.

"Trust me," she says, "she likes to have a good time. Even if her family is batshit crazy and she's partly brainwashed. Shit, she had a kid out of wedlock; that alone should tell you about her commitment to religion."

"Good enough for me," Chevy says, as if it were something that would benefit him.

After a few more, Gina tells us they are getting ready to close up, so we pay our tab and Gina and I exchange phone numbers.

"I live downtown, so just tell me when you're heading there," I tell her.

"I'll pick you up on the way. According to this guy..." She points at Chevy. "...you might pass out before you can walk out of your place."

"Damn, she's dedicated to getting you downtown," Chevy says. His point isn't lost on me, though again, I'm sure the comment is for his benefit only.

"All right, fine, pick me up. Here's my address; call when you're leaving here."

Chevy and I rise out of our coffins, and with a little bit of swerving, he manages to get me home in one piece.

"Remember," he tells me as I get out of the passenger seat, "I want details. Or call me; I'll come over and watch through the window if you get both of them back to your place and get them to make out with each other."

"I'll see what I can do," I mumble and shut the car door.

At home, I stand at the stove and pretend I have a choice—that fanciful choice to stop drinking, rather than the practical choice to start drinking vodka and Red Bull to keep the stamina rolling for later. I have this argument every night, but the result is always the same. Some say that is the definition of insanity: repeating the same actions and expecting the results to change.

I figure that being insane is probably the least of my worries, in the grand scheme of things.

I put on some music after pouring the drink and sink into my leather chair, the muscles in my ass and back thanking me with spikes of pain for subjecting them to the skeletal frames that pass for chairs on Houli's patio. I take a long gulp of pure caffeine and liquor, allowing it to collapse into my throat, stream into my stomach, and deconstruct into my bloodstream. Pretty soon, those spikes of pain can no longer be felt.

I only finish one drink before my phone rings. I look at the caller ID; it's Chevy, not Gina.

I flip open the phone. "Congrats on not wrapping your car around a telephone pole."

"I forgot—you *gotta* make it hurt a little, all right? With Gina. Or Maya. Just pull her hair or something, whatever."

"What?"

"Come *on*, man! What part of 'vicarious' do you not understand? I want to look at them next time we go get drinks and think about them getting nailed hard."

"Why would you want to think of me nailing them hard? What's wrong with you?"

"No, dammit—not *you*, specifically. Just the image in general. Oh, and hey—not too bad, just enough for that *good* pain. Slap her ass; they like that."

"*Good* pain...right."

"Okay, man. Remember, I want details. Don't black out!"

I close the phone. Luckily, before I'm left with any spare time that would force me to reflect on Chevy's words, Gina calls.

"Hey, we finished stacking all of these goddamn chairs. I'll be there in ten minutes."

"I'll be ready."

I put my shoes back on and walk into the kitchen, not even looking at the stove.

Gina drives an El Camino. I like the nostalgia of it. She has it decked out properly, a string of tassels across the top, a Virgin Mary statuette, and felt on the dash. It takes me back to when I was young and my uncle, my brother, and I would ride in his El Camino looking for hotel pools on the beach we could jump the fences to and go swimming in. It was a small thrill, doing something we shouldn't, but it was only simple trespassing. It was an innocent thrill, and I enjoy remembering that—an innocent thrill. Those have become rare as the years have gone on.

When I get in, she lights up a joint and passes it my way. I take a long drag, and she starts into a spiel about Maya.

"She's done some stupid things—she told me some things, but she's a good girl. That's easy enough to tell. Anyway, she's looking forward to getting out tonight. I figured Chillers would be good—lots of people her age. You mind Chillers?"

I look over at her. "I know I'm older than you, but I'm not fucking dead yet."

She laughs. "All right, good. Just saying, Maya and I might be dancing a lot so you will be on your own—"

"I think I can handle that," I tell her.

"And I don't want you to feel bad. Okay, okay. Anyway—"

"Hey," I interject, "I can't keep up with your million-miles-an-hour talk. You got some of that coke for me, or what?"

She laughs again and digs in her console with her right hand. I watch Boba Fett go rummaging and come up with a little baggie.

"Here you go. I have some other stuff for later, but this will hold you over."

I take the baggie. "You planning on an all-nighter?"

"Maybe," she says, pulling into the parking garage and grabbing a ticket from the dispenser.

Downtown is in full swing. It has dropped a few degrees more, so everybody is in jackets. Gina is wearing a denim jacket with patches on it. I've been drunk for hours, so I've forgotten a coat, but I still can't feel the cold. There are the girls in miniskirts and bikini tops braving the cold for commission trying to rope us into the club. We let them, getting our ticket for a free shot on the way in.

Chillers is a two-level club. The upper floor is a steel catwalk, and the lower floor is packed and dim with a colorful dance floor. We walk across the catwalk, and I look down at the floor; it's nothing but early twenties women dancing with the usual scattering of guys around the edges—guys whose best bet is to wait until the magic hour when the women are so drunk there are no inhibitions, but not so drunk they'd get puked on before making it to the bed. Learning that timing takes a lot of trial and error. I had the puke stains to prove it.

The music is thumping just a little too loud in my stoned ears as we meet Maya downstairs by the bar. Maya and Gina hold a conversation, but I can't hear a word of it. I order a vodka Red Bull while they talk and fuss, point at the dance floor, and laugh. I get my drink and theirs and then turn around. They both look at me with wide eyes as if I'd caught them in the middle of something. I look at them blankly and hand them their drinks.

"We're going to dance for a while," Gina leans in toward my ear and says. "Can you watch our drinks for us?"

"Of course," I say, barely able to hear my own voice.

They set their drinks down and disappear into the color and strobe lights. I lose them for a moment and then catch sight of them amidst the bobbing, strobe-lit heads. They are kissing each other and grinding closely, and I figure this evening is only getting better. Hopefully, Gina has some of that E for me.

While I hold the bar down and they dance, Chevy calls again. I flip open the phone and hold it up to my ear, putting a finger in my other ear. I have to shout just to hear myself.

He says something I can't hear.

"What?" I say. "You're going to have to shout."

"What?"

"*Shout*, dammit!"

"*Get any action yet?*" he shouts into my eardrum that is already pushing its capacity with the shitty dance music.

"*No, jackass*," I say. "If you want action so bad, come down here and get some your goddamn self."

"*You don't have to shout at me! I can hear you fine on this end!*" he shouts.

"*I can't hear* me *fine.*"

"*My wife will kill me if I come down there*," he says.

I close the phone and put it back in my pocket, and as I do so, a tan little twenty-something sidles up, smiles, and pushes completely up against me as she leans in to order a drink.

I'm probably too old for joints like this. Chevy was right. And his choice to be married and not be able to be here tonight is the right choice, and one I would make, I realize. But, at the same time, this young girl's warm, sweaty body feels good, so I just tell myself that whether it is choice or destiny that has put us all in our places, right now, my place in Maya's God's grand scheme isn't bad at all.

After about thirty minutes, and as many vodka Red Bulls as I can fit into that time span, Maya and Gina both come off of the floor and order rum runners.

"You two seem chummy," I say to them.

"Chummy? What's that mean?" Gina says with glazed eyes.

I keep forgetting about the age difference here. "Never mind," I say.

I turn to Maya. She looks at me, and I look at her. I'm undecided whether I should bother pursuing her or not, so I smile thinly. I could care less, but with the night begging for something to spice it up, it might just be worth trying. Even if the result is a simple story of failure, it's a result.

I turn to say something to Gina, and she leans in and presses her lips to mine and then slips her tongue into my mouth. I go with it.

"Is that what chummy means?" she asks after we detach.

I turn to look at Maya, not sure what I'm going to say. Instead of talking, she leans in and plants her full lips on mine, also flipping her tongue into my rum-and-vodka-numbed mouth.

I suppose a story of failure will have to wait, for now, but it looks like the results are in on whether the night is going to spice up or not.

Two minutes later, the three of us are sitting in a booth as far from the dance floor as possible. I am in the center of the booth with a girl to either side. We aren't sitting thigh to thigh, but our ankles and feet and shins are bumping against each other. I want to ask questions, but I somehow still have the good judgment to just shut the fuck up and enjoy the innocent thrill.

I feel like an El Camino, lazily cruising, ready to store memories in the back bed.

The waitress brings our next round. I notice these drinks are stronger than usual. Maya clears her throat and then looks at me.

"So," she says, "you're probably wondering what the hell is going on."

It's a rhetorical question, so I just raise an eyebrow and grin to say, *Ya think?*

"Well, we decided we both like you—we—us—all want the same thing; we want to have a good time, and there's something about each other that we like. So, why let stupid inhibitions get in the way?"

I want to bring up the religion thing from earlier in the night, but shut-the-fuck-up mode is thankfully still in effect. We still have to talk very loudly, though I am glad the thumping music is farther away, so shouting a question about religion seems like too much effort anyway. Instead, I ask the question that needs to be asked.

"You two are fucking with me, right?"

Neither of them bat an eye. They both look at each other and then lean across me and kiss each other; then they kiss me again.

"Okay, okay, I had to ask," I say.

The waitress shows up with more drinks, and we all sit back, sip, and light up.

"So," I say, "though I'm not quite sure what happened with you two, I have to say I like it."

"We were talking as we stacked chairs back at the bar, and the subject of experimentation came up. Things we've done, things we haven't. Shit like that."

Gina continues, "So we decided to do something totally off the wall tonight. We tossed some ideas around, but we eventually settled on one." Gina smiles as she says this and rubs my thigh. "Plus, I have some goodies to help the night along."

They both put down their drinks and tell me they are going to dance again. I tell them I'm going to hold the booth down; it's better to sit than to stand at a bar—if you already have someone to take home. It's even better if you have two. Gina slips me a baggie with two lines in it.

"Don't pass out on us now." She winks.

But it is only a few minutes before they return from the dance floor. They are both sweating and dig into their drinks healthily. The waitress comes back around, so I order one more round and say we want to close the tab. The waitress tells me there is no tab.

"Shit, really?" My eyes are wide in surprise. It's either surprise or the coke surging through my bloodstream, I'm not sure.

"Industry night," Gina says to me in explanation.

So we don't pay a tab and leave, heading back to my apartment. I'm unsure whether this is a choice that we have all made, or if it was predestined, but there is a part of me that knows after this night, I'm not going to be able to frequent Houli's for a while. I'm giving up my casket—another bar scratched off of the list. But it is worth it, worth the chance that this is by choice; I get to enjoy all of the pleasure for the next few hours and pay the consequences tomorrow morning all by at least semiconscious decision. Chevy might be bummed, but at least he'll get his story. It feels good just being along for the ride. All three of us pile into Gina's El Camino, three fluttering tumbleweeds on a buffet of booze and drugs, with religion relegated to an ironic afterthought, like the small Virgin Mary statuette on Gina's dash.

Racine

I crack open another bottle of rum and give the letter one more shot.

Dear Racine,
I am sorry. I'm sorry for the things I've said, the things I've done. I am sorry for the course we have taken, though we both know there isn't always control over that. I am sorry for winding up where I am, just like everybody else. Boring. Slowly dying and not even paying attention to it.

But we know what I am really saying. I am most sorry for the things I have not *said, the things I have* not *done. The paths I chose* not *to take. But they instill that fear in you so thoroughly, so completely. To choose can be so paralyzing. So, I didn't choose anything. And it led to a lot of broken promises, and that is why*

I drop the pen at this point and take another drink. The record has ended, so I flip it over and sit back down. I look through the window at the swaying palms, missing the pines and the snow and the mountains of home. On the wall next to the window is your imitation Warhol. It makes me smile; you always had a thing for Andy's art. All pop nostalgia really. I never truly understood your interest in the past, when to me it seemed that the future held so many more exciting things, so much potential to push the boundaries and create something *new*. Though that was part of the problem, wasn't it? I always looked toward tomorrow, toward what could happen, and never made a stand on the past or present—which meant that those tomorrows were never any different than the previous day. You called me a dreamer; I used to see it as a term of affection, but now I'm not so sure it was.

The weather is always nice here. I have a closet full of shorts and Bermuda shirts and sandals. It's paradise, and it bores me to depression. Sun, humidity, musky evening gulf breezes that numb your soul so that there is no joy to be found in the sun poking out in the morning; there is no joy in a pleasant evening. This town is full of parasites, all bred by the weather. The heavenly weather and low-key locals form an airborne disease, a disease that bakes your mind until no indiscretion is large, no loss is meaningful, no accomplishment is worthy.

I pick the pen back up and take another stab at the letter.

and that is why I am here, still, sitting with a bottle in my lap and my dreams of tomorrow and what tomorrow will bring. Though this town and its people have robbed me of the ability to effect a change, it does not mean that I have given up hope. Hope for us, yes, that is given up on. I am depressed, not delusional. And I am honest. I hope you always loved that about me, if not much else.

I pause again, thinking, and decide to stop for a moment. I watch the palms for a while and wonder how it was so easy for you to embrace this town, its people, its weather. It all stank of betrayal and deceit to me, from the first day, but I made the best of it. I got a job and wrote in the evenings, as you would paint and we would enjoy some Nick Drake and cocktails. Occasionally, we would speak across the room.

"How's the painting coming, honey?"

"It's forming. How's your story coming?"

"Shitty, you know how it is, babe."

And everything would seem right on those evenings; that simple, basic conversation was all we needed. Even the palms outside seemed right, a reminder of paradise in the dark, two souls peacefully lounging on a quiet night, together creating for that elusive tomorrow where something would be different.

I have to switch the record again, and it takes a little effort to pull out of the chair, but with a grunt and a few popping joints, I am able to walk over and change to an Explosions in the Sky record. It's one that we both loved, even though it was new by your standards. After setting the needle into the groove, I move to the kitchen to grab more ice for the rum, which I manage with very little swaying. I seem grounded tonight, at least physically, and don't have drunken sea legs yet. I'm hoping they show back up, Racine. I really am. Because when the world is shaky, it seems more right. It seems as uncertain as tomorrow, and that is what I need—a consistency in the entire unknown, just one consistency, even if the constant is that everything will be all shaken up and dizzy.

With the confidence in a dizzy constant and the melody of the record enhancing my mood to write the letter, I pick the pen back up.

> *I am sure you loved my honesty and maybe even some other traits. But as I mentioned, I know that I have become boring,*

> *paralyzed. I don't love this about myself, so it is hard for me to imagine you loving that about me. A dreamer that works to make his dreams happen is admirable. Or at least adorable in "the little train that could" way, even if those dreams never come to fruition. A dreamer who sits and drinks and does nothing... well, there's not much to love there, right? Something to pity, maybe.*

Something to pity. I have to stop on that line and take another drink. Because that was also what you had said—that I was a dreamer and then later, that I was something to pity. And it hurt because it was true. Not that I'd admit it, but it did. It stung with an unfamiliar ruthlessness that went straight to the core, unlike the swirling, sideswiping deviousness of the town itself. That just erodes you; it's a slow corruption. But what you said, that was an ice pick through my Bermuda shirt. And it was hard to forgive you for that, but since you were right, I couldn't stay upset at anyone but myself.

The town is full of drunks with nothing to do and lots of money to do it with. This is what most people dream about, but it is the worst cocktail you can imagine. It is a sleepy beach town where people have nothing better to do than plot against their neighbors and covet their wives. They don't covet each other's bank accounts, only the belongings that matter most to their neighbors, which is not money if you have real money. It's usually the intangibles. The odd thing about this town is that nobody desires power, which is usually what boredom and money lead to—at least broad power. They want, perhaps without even overtly knowing it, power over individuals in their lives, which is imminently more dangerous. Put an entire populace with nothing but time and money on their hands together, and this is what you end up with. It's a new definition of evil, really.

And you fell right into it. Dove, more precisely. Off of your nostalgic cliffs and into the eddy of secret wishes to choke the meaning from everything, to strip it, to leave it naked and wide-eyed. When your art changed, I said nothing. Your approach became minimalist; you said you were baring everything and boiling it down to its most basic elements. Portraits of neighbors became just a few hideous lines, and you presented them, wrapped, with a smile. It became something mean, something damaging, instead of something healing.

I pick up the pen.

You said that: "something to pity." I knew what you meant—know what you mean. But you forgot, in the midst of your accusations, to pity yourself. Because you became them—no, worse, you imitated them. You didn't have a silver spoon to truly disassociate from what you were doing, the havoc you were causing. And so, you joined their game, and you were consumed by it. And I am sorry. I am sorry that I let it happen because I was busy dreaming. Which is pitiful, but it also does not absolve you. Helping you back from the cliffs is one of those paths I chose not to take, and for that I am sorry.

I pick up the bottle and sit back. I don't want this to get accusatory. Maybe I shouldn't write this letter at all. We are all guilty of many things; the entire world of people is guilty of many things, so why should either of us be blamed for mistakes we made, people we hurt?

But, Racine, you did pay, and I will pay. You for what you did and me for what I have done. I can say that I am sorry, but that doesn't change anything; that is just the way of the world. If we were truly one of this town's bored elite, we might be able to buy our way out of paying. They certainly would have no conscience. But that is not us. You are free of conscience now, and I get to explore mine. For the one choice I did make, for the moment I broke out of paralysis, for the one time I made a stand in the present because of a recent past.

> *And now I get to climb your cliffs; it is the climb of atonement, and I will never reach the bluff. I know this; I am not delusional. I am a dreamer, and I will dream of that day I do reach the top of the cliff, to crawl up on it, and stand, and look out over the sea and see what you saw. It is a new dream. Because you betrayed the old dream. And soon they will find your body, lifeless in the bedroom, and they will find me, here in my chair. And that is when I will no longer be sorry, I will no longer feel the fear they instilled in me, and I will begin the climb. Up a snowy mountain, through the pines, to the cliff where you once stood and looked down upon all of us.*

Better Than Disney World

What possessed the landlord to finally fix up the place, I had no idea. The structure hadn't been repaired in ages. Yet, its aura was selfish and proud. I did not feel at home on my own rented floor, and I think the house had a part in that. It was an old place, and if you paid close enough attention or if you wandered too close from the street, you could tell it was a mean place. A cruel place. It drained you in ways that were imperceptible. It was a blight on the neighborhood and outwardly begged for modernization. But, inwardly, as an entity of its own, it had no desire to let go of its past.

They took an industrial sized dumpster and placed it right in the middle of the yard in preparation for fixing up the house. It was a massive hulk, the ultimate eyesore. The rusted container stood almost chest high and was so large it took up most of the front of the place. Not that I lost any sleep over it. But Roxy, the hooker from next door, would complain about it every chance she got. Somehow the gaping tub offended her. Or maybe it was just a reason to wrench my ear since I'd never paid her for sex. I guess giving it to me free left her feeling entitled to nag at me, which forced me to remind her that I was not her husband.

"Just look at this thing," she'd say as we lazed up on my porch, watching traffic pass by the disaster area of my yard.

"What do you want me to do about it? I didn't put it there," I'd say.

"It's completely unacceptable." Roxy, at least when she was with me, seemed to go out of her way to appear proper. I knew she had the mouth of a sailor, but around me, she never used it.

"Maybe you're threatened by it."

"How does a fuc—how does a dumpster threaten me?"

"Now there's something wider on the block than what is between your legs."

After a classless comment like that, I'd get slapped. She had a little bit of a temper; I figured it came with the territory.

My landlord, like any landlord, was a cheap bastard. So he hired a few vagabonds to do the windows and supplied them with the dumpster. The gypsy workers, Mick and Gavin, didn't bother me much. They were nice enough when asking for a cup for their beer or if they could store their suitcases under my stairs. I'd been there; I understood that. One of my neighbors had thrown out an old mattress, and the gypsies had pulled it from the side of the road. When I'd get up in the morning, it would be laid out in the grass, but those gypsies were already hard at work somewhere out of sight. They were elusive.

So, most days, we'd sit on the porch and watch the house supposedly change.

"Which one is that?" Roxy asked, nodding at the figure who had just appeared from the side of the building.

"Mick," I said.

She turned her lip up in contempt and sipped her beer.

"What do you have against these guys anyway?"

"Besides catching them spying on me in the bath, you mean?" she said.

"Sure, besides that."

"You can't trust gypsies."

I laughed. "But you can trust whores?"

I got a turned-up lip from her and nothing else.

"All right," I said, "tell me why you can't trust gypsies."

"They prey on old folks. I'd strangle those two if I could."

I shook my head. "Come on now."

"You haven't heard of the scams? They come down from Georgia as 'contractors' and drive around neighborhoods going door-to-door, saying they've just done the neighbor's house and have all this leftover tar, or whatever. They offer a discount, saying they don't want to drive all the way back to the shop with a half-full tank. Retirees can't pass up a deal, so they do the work, and the next time it rains, the spray paint they'd laid down washes away. My parents lost five hundred dollars to gypsies like these fuckers." She nodded down to the front yard, as if the bin represented them. "And my parents can't afford losing that kind of money."

"Hmm," I said. "Well, I hope they don't replace windows the same way, or next hurricane season, I'm fucked."

"Yeah, you hope. Good luck with that. I see a bunch of scrap wood piled up in that bin, but I don't see your place looking any different."

"They're doing the back first," I said, assuming they were. Mick had just come around from there.

"I don't hear any loud noises. Ripping out old window frames would make a racket."

"Maybe they're magic, silent gypsies."

Roxy set down her empty beer and stood up. "I'm glad you're not worried about it. I'd lock up your valuables though. Maybe even your nonvaluables. You can't trust those people." She started down the stairs.

"Big date tonight?"

"Fuck off."

Roxy wound through my yard and over to hers, keeping a wide berth from Mick, who was fiddling with an old window frame by the dumpster.

It was a Saturday, so no work. I was doing pest control again; I liked the driving time to myself but hated the sales part of the job, so I never moved up the chain. Kind of the opposite of the Irish Georgia gypsies. I'd rather just shut up and do the work than sell; I hated the sell but admired those who had the gift. Hell, if I could pull off the cold-hearted sell, I'd be ripping people off too. Start up some kind of self-improvement infomercial or something. Those guys all had the boats and women, until they got busted for fraud or tax evasion. I could probably pull it off though, my beer said to me.

I leaned myself back on my chair and watched Mick disappear around the corner. I had to admit they worked pretty quietly, which was strange, but hell, I wasn't paying their salary.

Inside, I heard the phone ring.

"Got the day free, family is doing one of the parks today. Up for beers?" Chevy asked.

"I'm busy watching the mammoth bin in my front yard," I said, "in case it decides to sneak away."

"Right. I'll be over with a twelve in a bit."

"All right. Get smokes too."

"Shit," he said in agreement and hung up.

Chevy arrived with perfect timing; I was polishing off the last of my beer and smoking my last cigarette.

"Lifesaver," I said to him as he walked up the stairs.

He threw me the pack, which I began opening as he stored the beer in the fridge, grabbing us both one.

"Where's your wife?" he asked, meaning Roxy.

"Hot date tonight," I said.

"Too bad. She's easy to look at."

"She's easy, period."

"What's up with the window gypsies?" He looked left and right down at the yard, unable to see a sign of them. "They've been here for a month, and I don't see any new windows on your place. Do they do anything besides drink beer?"

"No idea. They're working around back, I think. Mick, the short one with the long hair, was out here for a second when Rox was over here. Then he went back thataway." I pointed with my thumb behind me.

"Think he's got something for Rox?"

"She did tell me earlier that they've been peeping into her bathroom window."

Chevy laughed. "Creepy. She should move to the second floor."

"That would work," I said, "then all I'd need was a cheap pair of binoculars to get a peep. I can't see shit from this angle."

"Yeah," Chevy said, leaning back in his chair. "So, how's the bug-killing business?"

"Sucks."

"At least you get to tell people you kill things for a living. You ought to try sitting in a cubicle for eight hours staring at a fucking computer screen. That's what I tell people I do: stare at a screen for eight hours. That ends any more questions into my line of work. I hate talking about that shit."

"Good conversation killer."

"It's necessary to keep a few of those in your pocket."

"Always," I said.

A few beers later, Gavin and Mick popped out from some magic portal that apparently was at the side of my house. They were both wiry and tan. Gavin had a bald head; Mick had long, scraggly hair and was nearly toothless. Chevy and I nodded at them when they showed up beneath us.

"Just relaxing, nice day for that," Gavin said rhetorically.

We just nodded at each other, to say that yes, it was.

"You guys need a beer?" Chevy asked.

The gypsies looked at each other and then us. "Sure."

Chevy went inside to get four beers.

"Say," Mick said up to me, "you got a cup I could use?"

I yelled inside to Chevy to grab a cup. He threw the beers and cup down to them. Tops *ffwwwissted* off. Gavin guzzled right away; Mick took his time pouring his into the cup. Then we all raised our beers to each other, and they disappeared again.

"What's up with the cup?" Chevy said.

"He must have class. Between them and Roxy, I'm surrounded by it," I said.

We sit and drink for a minute. "So which park did the family hit?"

"Disney," he said.

"That's a three-hundred-dollar day, right there."

"Easily."

"I guess the free time is worth it."

"I guess," he said from his pocket.

A short while later, a shriek from across the street startled us.

"*Motherfuuuuuucker!*" it screamed. I recognized Rox's voice.

"Jesus, what now?" I said, as Chevy and I quickly got up and went down the stairs and over to Roxy's. She was standing at her bathroom window, pointing an arm at Gavin and Mick.

"I'm going to fucking kill you!"

Gavin and Mick just stood there, looking shocked. Or stupid. Or unconcerned. Roxy saw us approach.

"Kick these cocksucking gypsies' asses!" she said.

Chevy and I both stood there drinking our beers. In fact, all four of us men just stood there. She was naked and wet from head to toe. She was definitely easy to look at.

"Why would we do that?" Chevy finally asked and put up his arm to deflect the bar of soap that Roxy threw at him. It landed in the grass with a small thud.

Roxy shot an incredulous look at him and then me and then all four of us. In the background behind her, a trick showed up with a towel wrapped around his waist. "What's going on?" he asked.

"Shut up and get back in the bedroom," she said.

"This is completely unacceptable! I'm calling the cops!" she yelled at nobody in particular, attempting to regain some composure.

None of us moved an inch.

She turned her lip up at us, slammed the window shut, and pulled the drapes.

"Show's over, gentlemen," Gavin said. We all laughed.

"You know, she does have a problem with you—" I said, and before anybody could say anything else, Roxy appeared from the back of the house naked, wet, and carrying a large kitchen knife in her hands, lip in a permanent sneer. Not a vision of class by the longest stretch of the imagination.

"You guys better run," I said.

Chevy and I stepped aside as Gavin and Mick broke into a run toward my lawn. Roxy didn't let up; she kept after them.

"Shit," said Chevy.

"Yeah, doesn't look like she's fucking around."

We both took off after the gypsies and the murderous naked whore.

Seconds later, Mick and Gavin had crawled into the bin. Roxy circled the large dumpster; the ogling gypsies were holding planks from broken window frames in front of them for possible defense against the knife. It was three skinny, tan people enacting a prehistoric hunt. Or *I Spit On Your Grave*.

"C'mon, you faggots! Just one of you get out and see what happens! Or do you only like to look at women without them knowing about it? Scared to come out and face one?" Still wet, naked and angry, muscles tensed, she looked more like a sexy hurricane than a crazy hooker. Or she looked like a vicious cave woman, which somehow also managed to look sexy.

"Rox!" I yelled. She ignored me.

"Rox!" I yelled again. "Put down the knife. Fuck this."

She stopped taunting the gypsies but continued circling the container. Gavin and Mick kept the boards in their hands. She wasn't dumb enough to crawl in after them, and they weren't dumb enough to get out.

"Rox, it's not worth it. Come upstairs and get a towel around yourself. Have a beer, fuckin' relax. Chevy can take care of your, uh, friend in your house."

"I can?" said Chevy. I snuck him a *shut-the-fuck-up* look.

"Listen," Roxy said, still staring down the gypsies, "I'm not leaving here without satisfaction. They *owe* me!"

"Satisfaction?" Mick said. "Who do you think you are, some Miss Priss living down on the plantation? You're a goddamned whore!"

"I de-*mand* satisfaction, *Miss Scarlett*!" Gavin said to Mick with a Southern gentleman's accent, and they both started laughing.

I turned to face the bin and punched Mick square in his skinny jaw. He fell back into the bin. I pointed into Gavin's face, "One more word out of you fucks and *I'm* taking her knife and coming in there after you, you understand?" I could feel my eyes bulging out and my neck throbbing, though at the same time I couldn't be sure why I was so incensed.

Gavin just nodded his head, and after a moan, Mick stood back up, holding his jaw.

"They're going to pay for what they did! They ruined my trick! And their kind *owes* my family!" Roxy continued to shout at them, although apparently not directly addressing them.

Gavin and Mick looked at each other, thinking, *Huh?* But they didn't say a word. It looked like somebody was going to have to diffuse this situation; it wasn't going to diffuse itself.

"All right," I said. "Mick, Gavin, how much cash you got?"

Eager to get the crazed, knife-wielding woman away from them, they both replied in unison, "We got paid yesterday."

"All right. You got...six hundred between you?" I asked.

"Six *hundred*? Fuck *that*!" Gavin said, and Mick elbowed him. Gavin looked down to Mick's jaw, which looked a little crooked.

"Well...you know what I mean," Gavin said in a small voice.

"Trust me, Gypsies. Six. Hundred. Or she's going to stay here all night circling this goddamn trash bin, for reasons you don't even want to know."

They both looked at each other and then at Roxy and then at me.

"Yeah, we got six hundred," Mick said. "But for that, we get a piece of that ass too!"

Roxy screamed and started crawling into the bin. I rushed over and pulled her off of it, her showered but already sweaty body slipping out of my hands easily. But she did not try to crawl back in.

"That was strike two. Don't push it. Throw six bills over. I'm not going to tell you again."

The gypsies looked at each other and then me darkly. With dramatic reluctance, they threw six one-hundred-dollar bills out of the bin at Roxy's feet. Roxy picked them up and walked up to my place, but not without giving them the evil eye. Once she was inside my place, I told the gypsies to get out of the bin.

"You guys better disappear around back, or wherever it is you go. And one more thing: if you look into her house again, I'll have the cops down here inside of thirty seconds to check your licenses for the work you are supposedly doing here. How good are the odds that at least one of you has an outstanding warrant?"

Without a word, they crawled out and took their magic portal around the side of the house and vanished.

Chevy and I stood there, drinking our beers.

"Damn, your front lawn is *better* than Disney World," he said, tossing his empty beer into the bin. It made no sound; it was quiet. It had landed on the mattress, I realized.

"Listen," I said, pulling two twenties and a ten out of my pocket and handing them to him, "go over to Rox's and give that fool in there this."

Chevy looked down at it. "I thought you didn't pay her?"

"Yeah, well, now I'm paying for sex I haven't even had."

"Just marry her already, you stupid ass," he said and walked off toward her house.

Upstairs, Roxy had calmed down.

"Thanks," she said. She was wearing a T-shirt and a pair of my shorts.

"Look, those guys are nomads. They make their living by staying under the radar. They need to avoid trouble. I don't think they'll be back."

"No, I mean, *thank you*." She looked at the six bills on the table and then at me.

I didn't say anything; I got it.

"Why don't I cook you some dinner tonight? Seven thirty?" she said.

"That sounds good."

She stood up to leave. I held the door for her. On her way out, she turned to me and said, "Funny turn of events, huh?"

"In what way?"

"For a while there at least, I was the predator. Preying on those goddamned gypsies."

I smiled. "Yeah, yeah, you were."

She kissed me. "You sold that pretty well. You should go into that kind of stuff."

"What?"

"That whole situation. You're probably the only person in history to get money *out* of a gypsy. Didn't know you were such a problem solver," she said.

I wasn't sure what to say, so I didn't.

"See you at seven thirty," she said and left.

The suitcases disappeared from underneath the stairs that day, and the gypsies were gone. The eyesore of a dumpster stayed for the remainder of the summer, but the house never did get fixed up. The landlord went through several more contractors, but it was always something. Maybe that house refused to be improved; maybe it liked its cruel fragility. It remained selfish and proud to be a stain on the neighborhood. Eventually, that pride led to its own destruction. That year, Hurricane Charlie ripped through the town, knocking out every window frame in that old house, and caused a lot of water damage. The landlord had finally had enough and sold the land. It took a while to sell, but it did.

I moved across the street into Roxy's house, and she quit the life for an office job downtown. We got hitched and pumped out a kid. So, Chevy and I sat on Roxy's front porch and watched them demolish that old house across the street, so that a new one could be put up in its place. The house was stubborn; when they ran the bulldozer through, it toppled in whatever harmful direction was possible. Several workers' comp claims came out of that job, much to the chagrin of the new owner. Sometimes houses are meant to be, meant to stay. This was one of them, and it didn't go down without a fight.

Revival of August

Oh, August. You could be about two years old now. You could be wearing tiny booties like your mother did, with a strapped sundress on, and could have multicolored hair we playfully dyed pink, or maybe purple. How much hair could you have? I'm not sure; I don't know about those things, but I have my imagination, and in my imagination, your fair hair is curled slightly at your shoulders. We'd wonder where the curls came from, and ultimately, we'd decide it was from my father. Your eyes would be blue; of that, I have little doubt. Recessive gene or not, that is a fact. Sorry—would have been a fact. You could be starting to put your first words together. I don't think I should wonder what those words might have been.

There is dust, August, snowdrifts of dust. It seems these days, I can't sweep enough to even make the illusion of shine peek out from beneath the allergy-prones' nightmare of a blanket. The broom just seems to congeal it in streaks across the hardwood. There are particles that choose to rise against their clingy kin, and in their escape, I sneeze and the cats sneeze. The cloud never seems to settle. These days are dandruff, and the only illusion I've managed to sustain is the one where I am calm and collected in the outcome we find ourselves in, an outcome where you do not exist, and by extension, neither really do I.

No, the terminology is wrong; I am existing. Existence is simple. I think the word I mean is *living—alive—being alive*? Yes, being alive. So, I exist but am not alive, at least in comparison to how I envisioned my existence with you and my raven in this life. I hope that was not confusing, I know you are young, carefree, and perhaps even selfish in ways. But that is youth, and I know as the years progressed, your giving nature would have prevailed; you would have been born with each side on your shoulder, speaking to you at each crossroads. Were you actually to exist, I would hope that you embraced that carefree spirit and carried it as long as the world allowed you to. Being carefree is rare, like beautiful things and love actually conquering all. Rare like the good guy winning, and rare like demons being put to rest.

I heard a song today on the way to work, a song where the singer earnestly belted with disregard for proper pitch or key: "I just want something beautiful to happen here, right now."

That sentiment rang loudly throughout the car, and I found myself playing the song again. Such a simple line that says so much, because he doesn't mean the simple beauty of a sunrise or a sunset, he means something that transcends beauty that can be registered at a glance. He means connection; he means true light. At least rest easy in your prematurely eternal rest knowing that such things do exist. I tell you this from experience. It is a tornado, a vacuum, and a shining light that encompasses everything to the point of utter surprise. Whether you are waiting to cross a street or ordering dinner or doing your laundry, that light can be felt and seen by all. Each revelation, or more simply, external recognition of it, is always a warm surprise. Though I am sad to say, even such beauty can be fleeting—much like a song, or a revelation. Perhaps nothing can stay encompassed by something forever.

I last told you I was clearing the runway for what life might bring. Had I known the amount of debris littering the takeoff path, I might have delayed my revelation to you. Tornados can leave an awful mess, you know. Know that there will be not footsteps without you in mind and no sunrises or sunsets that do not leave more clutter or wonder in their wake at what might have been.

Do not doubt that the wonder is polished to a shine. Do not doubt that the wonder is capable of making the existing sleepwalking illusions burst with life and song, if even for a fleeting second.

Perhaps your first word might have been, *"Love."*

Chivalry's Not Dead

Cloudy has a decent body, but her mind is gone. As she strips for the entire bar, we sit in the booth and watch, waiting for a bouncer to pull her off of the pool table. But neither the bouncer nor the douchebag she is fucking this week for coke show up to yank her down. As the song goes on and more of Cloudy's clothes come off, the slowly gathering crowd cheers her on.

"Take it off!" they yell. "Show us your tits!"

I'm indifferent—well, drunk and indifferent. But that is to be expected. Besides the fact that Cloudy has smaller breasts than I prefer, I'm half expecting Rommel to make a chivalrous move, but he's drunk also and not moving an inch. Kristina is sitting in the booth and not moving either, though she is unintentionally offering a play-by-play for Rommel and me.

"Oh no she didn't! She just did *not* take off her pants!" Kristina says. "Oh my god, she did."

The room is filling with patrons from the bar side of the place, and our view is starting to get obstructed. Cloudy's bra comes off. I'm surprised to see that her cup size is actually decent. Who would have thought those were hiding under her unimpressive tight T-shirts all this time?

"Is she a friend of yours?" the waitress asks, appearing at the end of our booth. Kristina nods yes. The waitress looks annoyed, but since we've been downing them quickly for a few hours, she is willing to leave us out of it. But she says that Cloudy will be thrown out as soon as the bouncers reach the pool table. I tell the waitress she'd better get her ass in gear with the drinks then.

After the waitress scuttles off, Kristina asks, "Are one of you going to go take her off of there already, or what?"

I say, "Or what."

"Damn it," she says, her voice beginning to rise. "You can't just let her do this."

"You're right," Rommel says to her. "*You* can't let her do this. Please go stop her." He takes a drink and looks at her, daring her to get out of the booth and challenge the crowd. But Kristina is far too timid to create a scene.

"You know she has problems," she pleads, looking at Rommel and me. "C'mon, go up there and get her off."

I laugh at her unfortunate choice of words and then ask, "Why doesn't her boyfriend stop her?"

"Yeah, right." She frowns. "That guy? He's not even on planet Earth. I saw her sneaking into the bathroom with him." She nods toward the back of the bar. "She's had more than her eighty-pound body should be able to handle. Even with her tolerance."

She says this disappointedly, as if Cloudy's weekend rituals still let her down. How Kristina doesn't see this coming every time, I have no idea.

"Chivalry is dead," she says, trying to give us guilt-trip eyes and then buries her face in her drink to avoid any further confrontation.

The waitress drops off the fresh round, plus some shots that she says someone bought us. We ask who bought them, but she isn't sure.

"They were ordered at the bar," she says.

We pick up our shots, look at them, and then sniff them. It smells brutal. We toast and down them. Then we all chase them with our drinks.

"What was *that?*" coughs Kristina.

Peering between bodies in the gathered crowd, I can see Cloudy is now down to just her panties. This could turn ugly, though surely some kind of security will step in and stop it. It crosses my mind that they are letting this go on longer than usual, and then I remember that I don't really care and drink my drink.

"Oh my god," Kristina says and puts her head down into her hand as Cloudy removes her panties and begins shaking her ass to each corner of the table while dancing.

"That can't end good," I hear somebody at the next table say.

Immediately after I hear that, some fool from the crowd decides to get on the table too and take his shirt off. Cloudy doesn't notice. He also takes his shoes and pants off by the time her ass shaking rotates to where he is on the table. She looks at him, startled. He begins dancing in place, in boxers and socks, apparently trying to entice Cloudy to join him.

Cloudy, as I have mentioned, isn't quite all there. She can be sitting with a group and take part in a conversation, but Cloudy is never really *all there*. There is a cord not plugged in somewhere; anyone attempting to connect a plug into Cloudy's open slot is brave to the point of stupidity.

Sure enough, Cloudy punches the guy square in the jaw and shouts, "*Rapist!*"

He falls off of the table, in his underwear and socks, and knocks his skull on the linoleum floor. He is out cold. Cloudy nonchalantly steps off of the pool table and starts dressing. The music stops.

"Oooh! Is he knocked the fuck out? By a girl?" she taunts the passed-out underwear dancer, standing over his limp body. Then she spits on him. This clears the crowd back, and Cloudy stands up and strolls over to our booth. The music kicks back on just as two bouncers strut in to find the passed-out human spittoon. The underwear man wakes up, holding the back of his head and groaning. The bouncers grab each of his arms and take him out to the sidewalk and dump him there. Cloudy ducks down behind the booth, and the bouncers look at each other and disappear to the back of the bar.

"Well, I guess that idiot boyfriend knows a thing or two about Cloudy after all," Rommel says. "She's capable of taking herself off of the pool table. And anyone else on it with her."

Kristina groans, still holding her head in her hands.

Cloudy slides into the booth next to Rommel, sweating. One bra strap is hanging off of her shoulder, and her hair is a mess.

"What?" she sneers. "That asshole was asking for it. I was just having some fun."

"We could see that," says Kristina.

"Oh shut the fuck up, you prude," Cloudy hisses and asks for a light for her cigarette.

The crowd has disbursed. We order another round, which comes with another set of free mystery shots, which go down a little easier the second time around.

"Where the fuck is Jeremy?" she yells, looking around the section of the bar. "Jeremy!" she yells in a shrill voice. "Motherfucker dares me to dance on the table and doesn't even show up to make good on his bet," Cloudy snarls. "That son of a bitch owes me fifty bucks."

Kristina again lowers her head to her hand.

Cloudy rolls her eyes and slides out of the booth with her drink. "I can't deal with this shit right now. I gotta find Jeremy." She heads toward the back of the bar, shouting his name at the top of her lungs.

Kristina moans. "Now I'll never get home."

"You can come home to my place and get a cab later," Rommel says, adding, "See, I'm chock full of chivalry."

We weave our way the two blocks to Rommel's pad without Cloudy or her steroid-ridden cocaine dispenser. Inside, we settle down with drinks, and Rommel rolls a joint. I fix up some music. Rommel's dog smells everyone's crotches and then settles at the foot of the coffee table with vacantly expectant eyes. Rommel's place is oddly decorated. His military plaques are on the walls, as is his sword from his dress blues. The art is decidedly war themed; I can see through to the kitchen where a navy flag hangs above the breakfast nook. While something of a stereotypical crazy ex-military type, Rommel is also often a voice of reason in a crowd. He's a born talker and a good people reader; just don't get him fired up about the war.

As the joint goes around, the issue of Cloudy comes up. Kristina is upset at her, understandably; besides leaving her without a ride, the two women couldn't be farther on opposite sides of the spectrum. Cloudy is flashy and loose; Kristina is quiet and conservative, and despite having a good body with huge fake tits, she is fairly ugly. Her skin is waxen, and her mouth is wrong. The features are just *off*. When Kristina's not around,

Rommel and I call her Mask. So as Cloudy has a decent body and a destroyed mind, Kristina has a decent body and a destroyed face—which maybe explains a lot about their dynamic together. They easily get laid in dark bars that pour strongly.

Rommel and I are still indifferent to whatever Mask is upset about, but Rommel tries to be a voice of sound judgment. Or he's talking just to talk; with the alcohol and pot, it's difficult to tell.

"Cloudy's a big girl; let her do what she's going to do."

"She doesn't know what she's doing," Kristina says. "I can't believe you were just going to sit there and let the bar run a train on her," she dramatizes.

"You're angry at the wrong people," I say.

After another round, the joint goes out, stubbed to a roach. We are quiet for a minute, letting the high take over. The dog scratches behind one ear. Mask just shakes her head to herself and says she doesn't understand.

"Haven't you done anything…crazy? Something you aren't proud of—or didn't care that others wouldn't be proud of?"

"Sure I have."

"Well, that's Cloudy, every minute of every day."

"Is that a good thing?" she asks.

"It can be," Rommel says.

A few moments later, there is a knock on the door. Without waiting for anyone inside to say a word, in stroll Cloudy and Jeremy. Cloudy is swaying, and Jeremy is barely fitting into his shirt and looking vapid. They are energetic, and both of the dog's ears shoot up.

"Hey, y'all!" she says, "I brought champagne!"

She waves a bottle of champagne in front of her. Mask sits up and looks happy, but it's an apprehensive puppy perkiness that says she doesn't know what might happen after this short moment of joy.

"I'll get some glasses for that," Rommel says. "Have a seat." He points at the couch.

Cloudy plops down next to Kristina, which leaves Jeremy to hold up the arm of the couch. I look at his shirt and can't imagine that a shirt that tight is enjoyable to wear. His eyes are glazed, and he has a permanent drug induced grin, but otherwise, he's not talking. Though it looks like his teeth are chattering in his skull, I can see them grinding through his cheek.

Cloudy giggles. "I *knew* you guys would be here. I told Jeremy that we were picking up some bubbly and heading over to Rommel's, because that's where my peeps are!" She laughs and hikes up her skirt. She puts the bottle between her legs and unwraps the foil from the bottle top.

Kristina excuses herself to the bathroom, and Rommel returns with glasses and a Department of the Navy dishtowel to catch the cork. The dog looks up at him, interested in the new guests but unsure of what the excitement is all about.

"You guys got my shots tonight, right?" Jeremy finally asks, in a surprisingly high-pitched voice.

"Those were from you? Thanks," I say, shaken out of my high a little from the sound of the couch arm talking.

"Yeah," Jeremy says, nodding. "No, I mean, yeah, from me."

I don't even know if he realizes he's having a conversation. I say, "Those shots tasted like ass."

"Yeah," he says, still nodding. "No, yeah. Yeah, I like those. Sometimes. They're good."

"Right." I turn away to light a cigarette and try to forget this buffoon is sitting near me.

I pour Kristina and Cloudy a glass of the champagne. Rommel pulls out his stash box and begins rolling another joint after rooting through the music collection and picking something out. Jeremy asks where the bathroom is and walks out of sight, which I am momentarily thankful for.

"So what did you get into after we left Pine Street?" I ask Cloudy. She smiles and pulls a packet of powder from her cleavage.

"Wanna snort coke off my pussy?" she asks, waving the packet back and forth.

Rommel and I both laugh with an unspoken decline, so Cloudy begins chopping out lines on the table, unfazed. Despite her many problems, outer confidence is not one of them. Cloudy doesn't rattle easily, which can be good and bad, depending upon the situation.

We all do a line, and Rommel passes the joint around. After a few songs on the stereo, I realize that for some time now, there hasn't been a Neanderthal in a constricting T-shirt next to me or a disfigured mannequin on the couch next to Cloudy.

"Hey, where are Tight Shirt and Mask?" I say, snapping my head up and side to side in an attempt to sober up for a second.

We three look around; Jeremy and Kristina still aren't back from the bathroom.

"What's a mask?" asks Cloudy.

"Nothing," I say quickly.

I reach down to pet the dog and realize that there is a bunch of piss in my bladder. I get up and say I'll try to find them. I stumble through the kitchen and hang a left. I start unzipping and realize that I'm in the guest room. In the dark. I snap my head up again to try to shake some sobriety cells around. I turn around and walk, not exactly in a straight line, into the bathroom.

Kristina is kneeling in front of Jeremy, his cock in her mouth. It takes a second for both of them to realize that the door has opened and I have walked in on them. At once, I see Jeremy's eyes open wide as Kristina instinctively bites down on him when she turns her head to see who has come in through the door. His eyes look like the dog's—vacant and expectant—and I realize that the pain hasn't hit him yet, but he knows it is coming. He yelps and bucks, and his knee accidentally hits Kristina in the chin. It knocks her head against the ledge of the bathtub. He doubles over in pain. Kristina's eyes close, and she collapses.

I am stoned; when I am stoned, I hate drama even more than usual. Cloudy stripping and punching some fool out wasn't drama to me. It's not drama unless it corners me and forces me to pay attention to it. And this was about as close to home as it gets without literally being in my home. As I watch the two of them, all I can think is *Goddamn, Mask really took Rommel's whole let-loose speech to heart.* Ten minutes ago, she was an anxious puppy who never risked anything; now she's possibly been killed by her girlfriend's man while giving him head in a bathroom. A small trickle of blood is starting to come from between Jeremy's hands, which are covering his crotch. Without saying a word, I turn around and walk back to the living room and sit down.

Everyone is looking at me.

"What the hell just happened?" asks Cloudy urgently, the multiple lines of speed in her veins hyping her up.

"You'll just have to see for yourself," I say and reach to grab a smoke as I mentally test the muscles around my bladder. I need to take that piss. I get up and walk out the front door. I hear Cloudy get up and run toward the bathroom. Rommel comes outside to piss also.

"Fucking in the shower?" he asks.

"Blow job on the toilet, a bitten off appendage, and a potential head trauma."

"Fuck." Rommel sighs.

"Yep," I say, shaking off the dribbles, feeling the sweet relief of an empty bladder. It's a beautiful night out. The palms are just slightly swaying in the dark, keeping the mosquitoes and humidity guessing.

Back inside, there is shrieking and a lot of thumping around in the bathroom. I look at Rommel. He looks at me. He tolerates drama much better than I do, but I can see he is edgy despite being stoned.

"It's your place, it's your call. What you want to do, man?" I ask him.

He just shakes his head. "Let me think for a minute." He starts rolling another joint.

Back in the bathroom, Cloudy is yelling something about blood and Kristina's head, and Jeremy is yelling what about his blood and he's never going to have kids. Cloudy starts telling him it is good he can't have kids because he's a cheater and he killed her best friend. It's a stoner's nightmare—blown out of proportion without an ounce of rationality. This is getting worse by the minute.

"Well, we can't have the cops here, or an ambulance," Rommel finally says, having gathered his thoughts somehow amidst the screaming from the back room. "We need them out of here, and I have an idea how to get that done. Go in my room. To the left is a trunk. I have some M-80s in there; grab them."

"M-80, like the firework M-80?"

"Yeah, grab those," he says, putting the leash on the dog and walking toward the front door.

"What the fuck are we supposed to do with these?" I ask once I get out front.

"Watch," he says.

He walks up to the corner of the house. The bathroom is toward the back and to the left. He opens the window of the guest room—the room I almost pissed in—and lights the fuses on three M-80s.

"*Police! Open up!*" he shouts, tossing the large tube fireworks into the guest room. "*This is the police! We know you're in there!*"

Rommel trots back to the lawn where I am with the dog. "Let's watch this shit go down in style," he says, lighting up the joint he had rolled.

The M-80s make several impossibly loud explosions. *Bam! Bam! Bam!*

Smoke starts coming out of the open guest room window. I hear scuffling and a bit of coughing and then the creak of a window in the back of the house opening. It takes me a minute to realize through the weed haze that it is the bathroom window. Tight T-Shirt is shouting, "*Run! It's the cops! What about Kristina? Hand her through! Oh fuck, it hurts to walk! Let's go! Go! Go!*" I hear a faint moan and recognize Mask's pitch of voice. So she *had* woken up. *"Pass her through, hurry up!"* I hear Jeremy saying.

"Fuck you, you cheating bastard!" I hear Cloudy shouting back. Even through this, she isn't fazed.

Maybe Mask had it wrong; it is Cloudy who is not on planet Earth with us, and Jeremy is just a by-product of Cloudy's caustic universe. Even a universe burning itself out needs a witness; what better witness is there than someone who isn't bright enough to form an opinion? Was Cloudy a genius?

I snap my head up quickly to sober up; I was lost in pot tangents. That slight breeze whips a little around my ears and up my nose, so I inhale the clean night air all the way into my lungs; it feels so good I could be levitating.

"You knew they'd run?" I say to Rommel, handing back the joint.

"What choice do they have but to run, other than to give up? Even though they are injured, walking into the arms of the cops seems unlikely. They are far too high to think rationally. Then again, so am I, so maybe I'm just lucky they ran and didn't stay. Who knows?"

While we wait for the firework smoke to clear out of the place, I ask, "Don't you have smoke alarms in there?"

"I kept stealing the batteries from them for my remote controls and never refilled them."

"Good thing, I guess."

"Man, those two girls are all kinds of fucked up. Two sides to the same crazy coin."

"No shit. But they'll be fine tomorrow. Well, maybe not that tight T-shirt-wearing douchebag, but Cloudy will be fine.

She's the one who walks through a minefield and comes out untouched, while everyone around her gets their limbs blown off."

"Like a hero in a movie?"

"Like a leper who's immune to leprosy."

We both get quiet for a minute. Then, before the pot takes us on a tangent that makes us analyze our own crazy coin, Rommel says, "I should have told Cloudy to lick that coke off of my dick."

"She probably would have punched you and spit on you for saying that."

"It was the chivalrous thing to say, but now it's too late," he says, and Rommel, the dog, and I walk back inside to the blood and smoke. There are empty, overturned bottles, and half-smoked cigarettes in the ashtray still burning. Drama always leaves a trail of blood and smoke behind.

Faith in Electricity

It is one hundred twenty-six degrees in here, and I have a lone lamp and a computer. An extension cord runs from my surge protector, out the door, down the stairs, and into a socket in the laundry room. If I get caught doing this, I'm out on my ass for sure. Unpaid rent is one thing; unpaid rent and stealing the landlord's electricity is another.

I walk into the dim kitchen with my flashlight. Empty bottles of various sizes line the stove top. A roach scuttles behind them when my beam finds it, so I send out a "*Sssssst!*" for the cats, but even they are too hot to get up and come running for a snack. I track down the bottle of wine and walk back to the computer.

I'm talking online with Faith. I am drunk and trying to pick a fight. I miss her. She knows intuitively that I am about to veer into SorryLand—my own intoxicated amusement park. Nobody's ever dared to purchase a ticket in thirty-five years, and here she was, manning the gates without even asking for a paycheck. It gets unsettling sometimes, having someone in your head like that.

"It's fucking blazing in here," I sweat to her over my keyboard.

"Open your windows," she says, as if I hadn't already thought of that.

"I'm fine," I type.

"Don't be a martyr," she replies.

"And what's your excuse for not being here again?" I say for perhaps the tenth time tonight. I know she isn't coming over, but the several rums, beers, and now a bottle of Shiraz in my unfed gut give me the courage to be an asshole. It's not a fight I want with *her*. She happens to be there as an outlet, and the drink allows me to take it out on anything but myself, which is where blame truly belongs—which is exactly what a martyr is supposed to say.

"We've gone over this," the window blinks at me.

My cursor sits ready to pounce and complete the rise to a fight, but I resign myself to not making sweaty love in this dark sauna of an apartment tonight. It hasn't been my day up to now; why should that change?

"But I would defile every inch of your sweaty, smelly body..." I trail off into pleasant thought.

There's a pause, and then she says, "It makes me wet thinking about it."

I wonder about this. Are her panties really drenched, thinking of rolling around in the dark, sheets sticking to us like adhesives, every nerve throbbing? Or is she placating me?

"Keep that dampness in mind," I say, figuring it didn't make any difference either way.

"Have some more drinks, and you'll forget all about it. Take some aspirin p.m., or NyQuil. With the rest of the wine."

That's my girl—telling me to drink more and drug myself to sleep.

"Trying to kill me off for some future life insurance payout? That's forward thinking," I say with my fingers.

"I love it when you get all sentimental. I'm just trying to kill you off in general. Good night, you sexy bastard," she replies and signs off.

With nobody left to bitch to, I think about firing off an e-mail to the power company threatening to burn them to the ground. Jail is air-conditioned; it'd be worth it. Instead, I have some sympathy for the parts inside of the computer and just shut it down before the whole thing melts.

I grab the bottle of wine and step out onto the porch. Somehow, it's slightly cooler outside. Even in the dead of summer close to the equator, the goddamn humidity feels better than the heat of my apartment. There might as well be a lava flow on the hardwood—I swear I see mirages along it through the glass door. I consider bringing a blanket out to the porch and sleeping on that, but the mosquitoes cancel that thought. The lawn is out because of the fire ants. In the winter, this place is enviable, but in summer, Florida is just a curse.

Out of options, I finish the wine and plop myself onto my bed. I lay alone and sticking to the sheets. Though I feel I might spontaneously combust, I've mixed my drinks well; I'm out in five minutes.

I wake up in the baking desert of my apartment. The sun is warming the outside of the house; the dark paint on stucco slowly absorbing the heat. My first thought is of how brutal it will be in here by midday. My second is of Faith's warm, soft breast, and my other brain springs to life beneath the sheet. But it's too hot, and as soon as it jumps up, it goes right back down. Hungover, I peel myself out of bed and move to shut off the alarm that will never go off. The digital clock face is completely blank, of course.

I run down to the laundry room to unplug my electric lifeline and roll the sixty foot cord around my arm, hoping Ms. Bailey, the landlord, hasn't seen it. I splash some cold water on my face, but it seems to have no effect; it is bath warm on my skin before I can even dry it off. I mope around, shuffling in shorts and a ratty T-shirt like a refugee in my own home. I pick up the cell, pay the electric bill, and get a noncommittal timeframe for when I can expect to emerge from the third world.

Easily bored of moping, I decide I have to get out of this place. Anywhere is better than within these four collapsing walls. I throw a ball cap on my head of hair that, ironically, looks like I've stuck my finger in a live wall socket. Definitely not qualifying as a sexy bastard, I slip on my sandals and close the door behind me.

There aren't too many people busying themselves this early on a Saturday. I take a leisurely walk down to the lake and take in the joggers and artist booths. The art is all chintzy, and none of the joggers are worth eyeballing much. I am sweating out the drink, and I know I'm ripe as the rotten milk in my fridge, trudging around downtown *au natural* with the homeless and the passing car exhaust. I pass by a few bar fronts, but none of them are open yet. Bored with all of this as much as the inside of my apartment, I figure at least the convenience store will have a cold six-pack I can enjoy on my porch.

The 7-Eleven is pleasantly air-conditioned. As I make my way back toward the coolers, people seem to take the polite sidestep away from me.

I'm *that* guy today.

I'm in line, six-pack and a forty-ounce in hand, disgusting the patrons in front of and behind me with my rank odor when I feel it coming.

I get that one acid heave that tells me I'm about to hurl all over the cute blonde in her nice dress buying bottled water, the magazine rack, and very likely, myself. I go a decade without throwing up from mixing drinks, and one night of drinking in a boiler pot changes everything.

I take two steps out of line toward the door, and it comes. The throat opens as if someone pried it, and there is no shutting it; those muscles formed from a lifetime of swallowing are useless. The acidic, metallic tickle starts back and down, far behind your taste buds, but you already know what the taste will be like.

It spews—not so much projectile as a red-wine-tinged steady dribble. It's a lazy eruption, like the feverish volcano that leaves its lava along my hardwood—a slow, deliberate, unstoppable river.

I bring up my hand to try to catch some of it, forgetting there is a forty-ounce bottle of beer in it. I drop that, and then vomit into that mess and on my shoes. This just doesn't seem to be my day, again.

There is that awkward silence in the store when the register stops going *cling!* and people take an inward gasp, holding their air because they know the next breath is going to make their stomachs also turn up. Everybody is thinking the same thing: we are one second away from an orgy of vomit here.

The bottled-water blonde in the dress covers her mouth with both of her hands.

"Oh my god! That's gross!" She valley-girl's the "gross" out real long, so it comes out as *"Groooossss!"*

I wipe my mouth, look at her, and say, "Who the fuck wears dresses anymore, anyway?"

I toss a ten on the counter and tell the clerk to keep the change. I shake some glass and puke chunks off of my feet, adjust my ball cap, and walk out. You could still hear a pin drop in there as the door closes behind me.

I'm almost home, already halfway through a beer to kill the taste in my throat, when I get ambushed by my landlord.

She comes completely out of nowhere. Had she been waiting behind a tree? Is she able to turn *into* a tree? I almost jump out of my dirty, sweaty skin.

"Jesus Christ!" I yell when she appears in front of me.

"Boo," she says nonchalantly.

"You can't do that to people, Ms. Bailey. I almost sucker-punched you!"

"You can't sucker-punch somebody if they have the drop on *you*."

"Hmm, you might be right." I take a sip of my beer.

"You smell god-*awful*," she says, bringing her forearm up to cover her nose.

"Been workin' out," I say.

Unconvinced, she lowers her forearm to say, "Was that an orange extension cord I saw this morning winding up through your door?"

I furrow my brow into a very painful look. "My door orange what?"

She looks like she is about to chide me when I let the pained inquisitive look morph into a concerned look before she can wag her finger.

"Are you doing all right, Ms. Bailey? You seem a little off today." Switching gears can be an effective tactic.

Easily exasperated, she throws her hands up. "Just don't do it again! And rent is still overdue, Black."

I scratch my temple and say, "Okay, then." My brow remains falsely concerned for her well-being. No doubt she knows it is a charade, but never change your story midstream.

She disappears, turning into a tree or whatever she does to vanish so quickly.

Upstairs, I've got power already. Ms. Bailey must have seen the power truck park here; something else she'd had the jump on me with. I smile at that and at the cool blowing air that slaps me pleasantly in the face. All of my clocks are blinking green numbers. It's like walking into a casino.

"Jackpot!" I yell to nobody.

I head straight for the shower and then down a few shots of Pepto. I almost feel human again. Maybe, just maybe, this could be my day yet.

Later, I wake up, having accidentally slept my day away. So much for that. I open one eyelid and feel a six-pack headache tugging at my eyes from the inside, but my stomach is settled.

I smell cooking and hear noise coming from the kitchen. I walk up behind Faith as she whisks something in a bowl and give her a kiss on the neck. I can see her give a half smile, and her neck retreats playfully from the tickle of my mouth.

"Hi," I say.

"Mmm, hi," she says sexily. She's in one of my old T-shirts and her panties and is working on a bottle of wine. It's one of my white work shirts, and she has no bra on underneath it; it shows just enough breast to drive me crazy. I begin to harden, which pulls some of the blood from my brain, and my headache settles down.

"You are amazing, and you don't even know it."

"Good. Now get out of here; this kitchen isn't big enough, and you'll just get in the way."

That's my girl, trying to kill me with good food. I grab a beer from the fridge and walk out to the porch. The sun is starting to set between the trees with their trunks shooting everywhere, and millions of leaves wave up around the power lines—an amusement park for squirrels and birds. I park my ass on a chair and lift my feet up to rest on the railing; I feel like everything is aligned, humming along like a refrigerator. I am a conduit, plugged back into the world.

The Ultimate Backfire

Another Tuesday, another night to be lost, and what better place than on a familiar bar stool? It's Lou's, about as dingy as you can get. Even the bottles behind the bar have grime on them, and the floor stinks of spilled beer and piss.

I hide in the corner, behind the coin game, hoping to blend in with the drapes. It's a dark corner; I figure my chances of drinking to blackout alone are better than usual. But drunks aren't good figurers, so of course I wind up getting accosted by the bar whore anyway. She sidles up with the jilted swagger you'd expect, head cocked to a side asking to sit, drink sloshing down the side of her bursting popcorn-bag jeans. You know the kind; they don't fit right around the upper thigh and make women's asses look like they're walking around with a dump in their pants. I resign myself to it; I nod at the stool next to me.

The bar whore, whose name I have easily forgotten, has heard through the slurred grapevine that I'm a writer. So she's showing me her smart side, which isn't saying much. She's not the brightest cube in the tray; everybody knows there are far more stupid writers than there are smart ones.

"Your glass is half empty," she observes, lighting up a Capri menthol.

"No," I say, "there is ice still in it. It is three-quarters empty."

"Hmph," she says. "So you're one of those."

"One of what." It's not really a question.

"One of those people who always find the worst in things."

"You're the one who just chose empty over full," I say.

Normally, I'd dodge conversation with her, but if she's ordering the drinks, I'll stick it out as long as I can. As long as I don't wind up pushing her off her stool, or worse, winding up in the sack with her, it's all good.

"Do you always avoid answering questions?"

"Maybe," I say, already annoyed.

"Hmph," she says. "Want a drink anyway, Mr. Negativity?"

"If you have to ask, why are you sitting here?"

"Because I like you," she replies to that which needed no reply.

"That's great," I say and slide my empty glass to the inner edge of the bar. I nod at Jeanne. "Keep 'em comin'." Her eyes tell me she knows what I mean. She looks at the whore. "Destiny?" Destiny nods yes. Best bartender in the world, she solved my empty-drink *and* my forgotten-name problem. Maybe even on purpose. Good old Jeanne.

"Do you like me?" the whore asks.

"Draw two boxes on a napkin and I'll tell you," I say, thinking that'll end that.

"Oh! Like in school?" She snickers and starts fishing a pen out of her purse. I take a look over; women's purses cease to be a mystery once men hit their teens, but I like to check for handguns anyway. Long story. She's rattling in there, and I see a compact, what I figure is eyeliner, a few singles, and some tube-looking thing with a nipple on it. She pulls a pen out and starts scribbling on a napkin.

You gotta be fucking kidding me, I think, though there is a certain appeal in her obliviousness. I bet she's real good in the sack. So much for getting sloppy alone, tonight was determined to do me in. *Do I have any condoms left on my dresser?*

Destiny slides the napkin over. It's folded four times, and on the front of the square is an inked heart. Cute. I open it up and hold the pen, hesitating. My instinct tells me to check the "No" box. Instead, I create a third box, under which I print "tonight," check it, and slide it over.

She smiles, folds it back up, and puts it back in her purse along with her pen.

"I've just unwittingly created a keepsake," I think aloud.

"Aww, that's so sweet," she says. I cringe.

Jeanne shows up with fresh ones and walks away. She might have been shaking her head to herself, I can't tell.

"Listen, honey, why don't you go play some tunes on the jukebox? No country though." I slide a five over. She pecks me on the cheek.

"Okay, sweetie."

I relish the few minutes to myself. It is, after all, what I'd come here for in the first damned place. I look around; it's all regulars tonight. I'm pretty sure every male in here has ridden the Destiny bike. I even imagine a few stare-backs that tell me, "Yup, buddy, I know."

I'm brought back to my unfortunate reality as Destiny plops her ass back on the stool next to me. It makes an odd Styrofoam sound, like when you pull an appliance out of a box. *Shhhk.* What's she got, bubble wrap in her back pockets? I notice that while she had been eyeballing the jukebox, she'd reglossed her lips. It works. I look a little closer; her tits are actually quite incredible beneath her too-tight Brooklyn Downtown T-shirt, and I've always had a thing for long red hair. Long red hair and great tits: trouble. I'm not even counting in the amount of booze in my system with that.

"I picked some stuff. Hope you like it."

Some boy band comes on; I hate it, of course.

"Yeah, that's great, baby."

She smiles and kisses me on the cheek. I cringe.

Closing time. We pay our tabs and head to her car. Jeanne gives me an odd look before locking the door behind us, but maybe she's just tired—or judgmental, whichever; Jeanne could get moody. My place is close, but Destiny drives us there anyway. We're sitting in the car out front of my apartment, looking at the ancient structure. It's not quite a century old, but it's home. Something of a monument on its own; it surely has enough history in it. How many people died here, fell in love here, fell apart here? It's not a bad place, from the inside out.

"Um, I gotta tell you something," she says, turning down the radio. I thank God for that.

"Uh-huh."

"Um…I have a yeast infection. I can't."

I raise my eyebrows out of pure instinct. Cunt problems usually make me do this. She takes it for concern.

"That's pretty forward of you, but I appreciate it, I guess."

"Ohh, I'm sorry, really. I really like you." She grabs my hand.

"No sweat, baby, I could use a blow job."

"Aww, you're so sweet," she says.

We laugh, and I almost want to marry her for that answer.

Upstairs, I fix us two drinks and put on some music. I need at least good music at this point. She holds her glass of wine and Capri and does a little dance in the hallway. She could move those hips, all right. Like a pro.

"Do a dance for me," I say.

"I thought you'd show me your writing." She pouts, still grinding the air. "You are a big-shot writer, right?"

"Maybe later. I wanna see a dance. No girl has ever danced for me. Not even the dancers." The line comes easy; it's true.

She walks over, puts out the Capri, and hands me the glass of wine. I put my rum down.

"Hold this," she says. "Put on something with a good beat."

I turn to the stereo to find something with a beat.

"Okay," I say.

She sexily smiles as the song starts. She has her arms above her head, straight out, and her hips cocked. Then she begins moving, slowly though, and the arms come down alongside her body. At about half time to the beat, she moves into a grinding motion. I catch a glimpse of one of those Egyptian-looking tattoos at the crack of her ass. Tramp stamp or not, those jeans are still bugging the shit out of me, but it's too late to worry about that. Her body is gyrating, and I'm fixated on that chest. That chest is no joke.

"Mmm," I say, not quite intending to. She moves closer, grabbing the wine glass out of my hand. Her legs straddle my knee, and it doesn't take long for me to get hard. Her hair is folded over to one side, draped over her breasts, which rise and fall beneath the T-shirt. I want to get it on with those tits. Put myself right between them.

"Hi," she says.

I finally have to smile; if tonight is going to do me in, this isn't a bad way to go.

"Hi," I say back.

She goes right down on me. I don't even make it to the tits; she's too good. No woman has ever made me finish that quick, especially after a lot of drinks. For a second, I'm even picking out the ring.

She goes to the bathroom to spit; I take a drink of my rum. Some other song ends, and I set the drink down. From the bathroom, I hear that noise again, *Shhhk*. It sounds like a plastic-covered couch being molested. I'm curious, but at this point, even zipping myself up looks like a waste of effort. Fuck it, maybe it's some sort of yeast-pumping machine; what do I care?

She comes out. "I need to lie down for a minute."

"Knock yourself out," I say, not wanting to move.

I wind up finishing my rum and a few more songs. It's good, better than a blackout, and being lost didn't seem such a bad deal at all. My glass was half full.

I zip up, get up, and walk to the bedroom. Destiny is lying on the bed with her legs propped up against the wall. There's a pillow under her ass. She smiles at me. I start to get undressed; the belt *sssslits* out, the shoes *dramp, dromp*, upon the floor.

"Tired from dancing?" I ask her.

"Yeah, getting fresh blood in the legs," she purrs.

"I can go again, you know," I say, not really 100 percent on that. It really could take too long. The rum was beginning to take its toll.

"Whatever you want, baby," she says. And I wonder what cut of diamond would fit her whore finger best.

My hangover is brutal. She's gone. I must have kicked her out at some point, or she slithered out; I'm not quite sure, nor am I quite sure I care. The bed is a mess; she was here for a while at least, that much is obvious. I wobble myself to my feet, call in sick to work, and look around the place making sure I still have a DVD player, a watch, and pets. All check. It's almost noon, so I head to Burrito Kitchen and wolf down a few tacos. Another Wednesday, another day to be lost. I've got nothing to do, I realize after eating. When you choose to spend a lot of time alone, that just seems to happen—you wind up alone. With nobody to call and nothing to do, I head back to the bar. That is always there.

Jeanne has to pull an early shift for the bartender who called in sick—another alcoholic, not that I am in any position to pass judgment. Jeanne sure does.

"Motherfucker, I'm supposed to close *and* open? You better tip well; I'm not in the mood for this shit."

So, Jeanne is in a good mood. It is just me and her; the place is dead. Not too surprising. No food for the lunch crowd, unless food consists of spirits or hops.

"Yep, sorry, Jeanne. I'll tip what I can." I wink at her. I dig in my pockets and pull out a lone twenty. How much did I spend last night? I add up the cost: five for the jukebox, a few toward the tab, and now a day of work off. Destiny wound up being expensive, and she didn't even rip me off.

"Yeah, well, don't sweat it. I'm sure you have other things to think about," Jeanne says, pouring me another beer.

"Things like what?" I ask.

She gives me a look I don't like. It's the one eyebrow raise. Instinctive.

"Ah fuck, what?" I say. It's not quite a question; it's more of a resignation. To what, I'm not sure yet.

"Have fun with Destiny last night?" she says.

"I suppose so," I say defensively, again not really sure why. Jeanne grins.

"Stop grinning like a fucking idiot already," I say.

"You know she wants a child right?" she says, her smile fading.

"A what?"

"A kid. Boy. Girl. I don't think it matters, really. She's looking to get knocked up."

"What?"

"She's looking for a sugar daddy. Even carries around a turkey baster in her purse and wears Depends to keep it in," Jeanne says, reaching between her legs and pushing her thumb up to her fingers, as if she had a syringe in them, "if she winds up sleeping with someone who is a good candidate, which doesn't happen often."

"What?" I say, but Jeanne knows she doesn't need to repeat herself.

"Fuck," I say, not quite intending to. I'm already picturing it: legs up on the wall. Destiny never spit it out; she spit it in. *Shhhk.* Depends. *You gotta be fucking kidding me!*

"*Fuck!*" A keepsake, I'd called it. Tonight: signed, sealed, and delivered. I lower my head. No getting out of a DNA test now. "You're the one who chose full over empty," I'd told her. "Knock yourself out," I'd said. Shoulda said, "Knock yourself up." Last night's determination to do me in wound up a success.

"Wait," I say, with a dim lightbulb above my head.

Jeanne cocks an eyebrow.

"You said *good* candidates. I'm broke as hell and haven't even been published in anything decent."

"Even a bad writer has more potential than most of the people in here," Jeanne says, making a sweeping motion to the empty room.

"As what?'

"Don't ask me; I'm just the bartender," she says.

"What is that supposed to mean?"

"It means, don't ask me to explain Destiny's motives." Jeanne gives me the same look she gave me on my way out last night.

"Sorry," she says and walks to the other end of the bar.

"Yeah, me too," I say to my three-quarters-empty glass. *The best bartender in the world probably would have warned me,* I think. I sink back into the drapes as some boy band kicks on from the jukebox. I am finally isolated.

Her Good Friend Bad Luck

Winter is starting to show itself. Though there are no trees here that shed their leaves, it can be seen in the earlier nights: the inactivity of the air conditioner and the thin sweaters pulled off of shelves throughout the city. People begin to complain that it is too cold—people who, a month earlier, were complaining it was too muggy and humid—but they walk now with a little more pep. Winter in the tropics wakes up the soul; it doesn't send it into slumber like the long, mundane summers, and people come out of hibernation. It is as if a blanket is lifted off of our heads here, and we all are a little sharper, a little more observant, and therefore, a little more likely to fall in love. Fall in the tropics is like spring in the north. As the end of winter is decided by a groundhog in Pennsylvania, the end of summer is decided by the lack of thunderheads and afternoon showers in Florida.

Faith and I are two of those people who have popped our heads out of the ground and decided to wander a few blocks to Dexter's cafe. People chatter around us with their drinks and cheese plates. Some faint jazz music can be heard coming from inside the restaurant. Somehow, the constant low hum of voices mixes perfectly with the offbeat, jerking jazz and creates a buzzing din. "Sit down," it says. *"Time to celebrate the end of things—the day, the week, the sleepy season."*

We are seated outside on thin metal chairs, but the chill cannot reach me through the seven-foot-tall heating lamp beside our table. Faith weighs as much as a newborn kitten, so she keeps on my blue Gore-Tex pullover and lets the martinis warm her from the inside.

"Y'know," she says between two bites of an olive, "I've just had this bad feeling all day, like something is going to go terribly wrong."

"Why is that?" I ask.

"Well, because for the past three days, everything has just gone...perfectly."

My eyebrows rise in curiosity.

She rolls her eyes. "Perfect. Seriously. Haven't hit a red light or spilled a coffee or blown up at work or even gotten a call from a bill collector. But I just keep waiting for the ball to drop. Don't you ever think that? That...How should I put it?...there is always *something*, always a stress or a worry or a problem or some reason to just chalk up another mindless nag or expense. Am I making sense?"

"Sure, I think everybody gets that. Though I never really pegged you as a pessimist. So what's the problem if everything is perfect?"

"I'm not sure, but it's the kind of small things, all built up, that just make me think I should be looking out for a meteor coming out of the sky and falling on my head. I mean..." She takes a sip as she gathers her thoughts. "...it's just been a constant stream. It's as if what should normally go right actually does, Murphy be damned. I can see a day of that as a pleasant anomaly. But three days? That just doesn't happen. It makes me worry—and, I know I haven't answered your question yet. What's the problem, right?" She takes another bite of an olive and then lights a cigarette before continuing.

"Well, I guess it might sound weird, but I always assumed everybody was like this; I think deep down, I don't deserve it.

Like some little cupid of luck accidentally hit me with his arrow instead of someone else, like in those comics where some chubby winged angel accidentally shoots a sheep and a farmer and they fall in love. I've always associated luck—*ongoing* luck—with the very rich, or famous. Obviously, I'm not talking about their kind of luck here; I'm talking about a few green lights, but something in me makes me wait, makes me keep looking over my shoulder for that inevitable boulder rolling down to crush me because I've used up all my luck in one three-day spurt."

"So you feel guilty for hitting a few green lights, basically," I say, leaning back in my chair and smirking.

She sighs. "I guess if you put it like that. Like, karma is going to catch up with me and see that I've racked up a huge debt with it."

I laugh. "No, it's not karma; it's guilt!"

"Karma," she insists.

"Guilt," I reply.

"Karma," she asserts again.

"When you say 'karma' is going to catch up with you, you mean 'God.' It's guilt."

She thinks for a second, and I imagine her next words to be "*Karma, infinity.*" Instead, she just grabs a piece of Brie and leans back.

"Call it what you want, but I'm sleeping with one eye open tonight, in case the roof falls on us."

"You're such a Catholic," I say and pay the tab. We walk home in pleasant weather. We do not have to stop at the crosswalks for any cars, and we get an immaculate night's sleep.

We have our traditional Saturday-morning coffee-with-crossword breakfast and then begin getting ready to drive to the coast. There's a casino boat, the *Ocean Princess*, which leaves out of the port in a few hours.

"You'd better bring all that luck with you!" I yell to her as she changes.

"The boat is going to sink, you just watch!" she yells back.

The toll roads give way to one long, vastly boring stretch of highway that heads right into Port Canaveral. The forest that lines it is a tinderbox, so we are careful not to throw any butts out of the windows. The traffic is moderate; the cruise ships stagger their port days, and there is no shuttle launch planned just north in Cape Canaveral, so it's a pleasant drive. The sun is up, and it's only the slightest bit crisp.

"It's freezing," says Faith, predictably. "Turn off the AC."

"Getting a little nippy?" I ask and move my eyes down to her chest.

Instead of getting shy about her hard nipples, she thrusts them out and turns toward me.

"Turn off the AC, or I'll shoot!"

I comply, turning off the AC. We ride for a few miles, smoking and playing with the radio. After about fifteen minutes, I look in the rearview mirror and notice there's a state trooper right behind us.

I slow down and get into the right lane; checking my speedometer, I realize I'd been speeding, but not much more than ten over the speed limit. On a highway in Florida, or at least on this one, that's usually a free pass.

"See?" says Faith, confident that her usual luck has finally caught up with her. The cop pulls behind me again and this time flashes the lights and hits the siren with a little *whoop-whoop*.

"Sonofabitch."

I pull over to the road's shoulder, gravel spitting out from under the tires and into the tinderbox forest. I tell Faith to go in the glove box and get my papers as I roll down my window and do a quick mental check: seat belts on, contacts in eyes, not drunk. Good to go.

Seconds later, there's a tapping at the passenger side window. Faith rolls down the window.

"Hey now, y'all. Keep them hands where I can see 'em."

"Hello, officer," I say, leaning over Faith to get a look at him, my hands on the steering wheel. He is large, with a bushy mustache and dark aviator glasses. He also has the state trooper hat on, which resembles a cowboy hat with a flat brim. We just got pulled over by the greatest cliché ever.

"Y'all in some kind of big hurry there?" he asks.

"No," Faith says. "Were we speeding or something?"

"Well, I got y'all at seventy-two. That's..." He looks at his pad for some reason. "...seventeen over the limit there."

I think, there *where*? There *here*? *There* was no way in hell I was going seventeen over, but in the interest of getting to the boat on time, I decide not to pull out my Fuck Authority card.

"*There's* no reason, no hurry," I just say. The inflection of sarcasm is lost on him.

"All right then, let me see y'all's license and registration and proof of ins-ur-ance." Faith hands these to him. He takes the papers and walks back to his squad car.

"See! See!" says Faith, grinning at her victorious prediction that something would go wrong and therefore right the universe again.

"You're smiling while I'm going to have to do online traffic class and pay a few hundred bucks because Gomer Pyle *there* can't read his speedometer correctly?"

"It's just nice to be back to normal," she says, slumping a little in her seat because I am not sharing her enthusiasm at being harassed by a lying cliché.

I'm not really worried about the ticket though. As long as I get to gamble and don't have to sit in a cell all day, I'm all right. Hell, I'll win back the two hundred bucks this ticket will be. Easy.

"All right now, y'all," the trooper says, back at Faith's window, "y'all look like good people. Goin' tell y'all what; I'm not goin' get y'all for speedin' there." He pauses after this, as he's doing us a favor from his point of view, and we are expected to do a high five or something. But we just sit there, one of us gleeful yet pouting and one of us indifferent and impatient.

"Okay," I say to him to break the ice and get things moving.

"But listen here," he continues, handing the paperwork back to Faith, "that there ins-ur-ance card is expired. Now, I could do a lot, but like I said, y'all look like good people, so I'm just goin' write that ins-ur-ance up on a ticket, and you send in proof y'all covered and seven dollars. That sound all right with y'all there?"

No longer fazed by the grisly slaughter of language, I just reply, "Yes, thank you." We get our seven-dollar ticket, and the cop pulls off before we do.

As we pull off of the shoulder and back onto the highway, Faith laughs.

"We look like good people!"

"He meant we looked white," I say.

"Yeah, probably. But, hey, I don't have to worry about the gambling boat sinking now."

"Because we got pulled over?"

"Yep!" she says, beaming again.

"I don't know about that. I would say that though we got pulled over by a subtly racist Captain Mayberry *there*, we did still get out of it with a seven-dollar ticket. Shit happens, but a seven-dollar ticket? Unreal!"

"Hmph." Faith shrugs, now unsure where her luck stands at all, which I find harmless and cute.

To get to the port, there are several large bridges to go across, of which Faith is afraid, so she closes her eyes tightly every time we go over one, but finally we reach the flats and then the exit to the terminals. We park and join the others walking onto the boat: old couples, vagabond types, and a few young people with stars of jackpots floating in their eyes. We fit right in, and once on the boat, we work our way to the top deck to the outside cabana bar. As soon as we have drinks in hand, we move to the railing to smoke and are surrounded by flies, but at least there's a nice sunny breeze. The breeze is always better at the coast, and despite the change in temperature, Faith decides that she is not freezing.

The boat lets out a foghorn sound and then moves away from its moors. The water in Port Canaveral isn't much to look at; it's muddy and dirty with various Styrofoam containers floating by. But this does not bother anyone aboard; they've started playing Caribbean music over the speakers, which puts everyone in a festive, spending mood. *It's a vacation*, the music says, *even if just for a few hours*. Faith and I make sure to hit the bar often. The casino will not open until we are in international waters, which is about a twenty-minute trip out, so we smoke and drink and Faith talks with a few of the old couples around us doing the same. None of the old people seem bothered by the flies, I notice.

Eventually, we hit the international boundary, and we wander below deck to begin gambling. We start at some traditional slots, which swallow our quarters with ease, so we move on to the video poker machines. Though it is only an illusion, the idea that poker is partly a game of skill makes the idea of winning on these possible. But they have added side games that are irresistible, things where you can carry over your win and hope you hit at least two pair on the next hand for double or nothing. I lose my ass slowly, but Faith has begun to build a small fortune getting lucky on double- and triple-ups. Soon, she's parlayed twenty bucks into a hundred and forty. Another two pair comes up, and she turns to me.

"What do I do? What do I do?" She's excited, naturally, and has that gambler's spark in her eyes, which makes me realize no matter what I say, she's going for a quadruple-up. So I tell her what she wants to hear.

"Do it!"

She does it, wins, and lets out a *"Whoop!"* that helps me forget the seven-dollar ticket sitting in my glove box.

"Niiiice!" I nod, and we trade high fives.

A minute goes by, and I lose the rest of my change, but Faith is still on a roll, working with a two-hundred-plus account on the machine. I think about telling her to start playing it safe and withdrawing occasionally but then decide against it. Not only has balls-out betting gotten her ahead, but only a fool walks into a casino expecting to win, so even if she loses it all, it doesn't matter.

I throw another twenty in, deciding it will be my last for the machines before hitting the actual tables. Beside me, Faith is rolling higher and higher, now up to three hundred and fifty dollars.

"How much have you put in?" I ask.

"Forty," she says without averting her eyes. She has the fever, and there is no reason to tell her to slow down. She is intent on the machine, watching the LCD cards pop up. She hits the screen with passion and focus.

Another double-up hits. "Four-oh-five!" she yells, throws her arms up, and then does a little victory dance in her seat.

"Y'all got it goin' *on* there!" I say to her, imitating the cop who'd pulled us over. She laughs and pecks me on the cheek. I return the favor with a playful smack on her ass.

"Go ahead and hit the tables. I know you're dying to play a *real* game," she says, content to find her video poker destiny without me.

"Thanks," I say, "though I doubt I'm going to surpass your virtual winnings." I get up and wander over to see what table games they have. I find a Caribbean Stud table. It's explained to me that the game is a mix between poker and black jack; I am playing against the house.

I set twenty in chips out. The pocket is dealt to me, AK unsuited, with a queen dealt up. I'm told I get to choose to check or bet. The idea here is pocket pairs, I see. It's a tourist game, not a real poker player's game. But it can probably be worked.

An hour later, I'm up about a hundred fifty as Faith appears at my side, beaming. I hand her a drink I'd ordered for her just a minute before; telepathy can be a dangerous thing.

I look at her and smile, expecting the worst, "All right, how much, big shot?"

"Five."

"Hundred?"

"Thousand! I just doubled up every time; it was ridiculous. I hit a royal flush on the last bet."

"Damn! What? Damn!"

"Let's just say I'm still looking over my shoulder for that meteor to shoot out of the sky and disintegrate me!" She laughs.

"With that kind of luck, I'm surprised you don't have meteors shooting out of your ass. Come rub some good luck all over me, baby."

She gets up behind me and puts her arms around me. I double up the bet; the deal comes: win. I'm now up three fifty, which makes it a comfortable bankroll to start playing aggressively. Aggressive can be good or bad, but with Faith on my arm, I can't seem to lose. I drop a few pots here and there, but I'm lucky enough to bet low on those. The ones I load up on, I hit.

"This is fucking ridiculous," I say, sliding a five chip to the dealer as a tip for another pot.

"C'mon, let's go eat. I'm hungry."

I don't really want to get up, but the idea of relaxing with a drink never sounds bad. I rack up my chips, and we walk down to the restaurant level. She orders nachos and a chardonnay; I order a burger and a Captain and Coke. It sounds like a disaster, but it goes down well enough.

As we finish eating, the voice comes over the ship's speaker system saying that the games will close in fifteen minutes. We have begun our return trip. Faith and I down the rest of our food, pay, and head back up to the table games. We wander the floor for a while, trying to decide where to place our money. The tables are winding down; the old people have retired back to the top deck to wait for the flies, so there are plenty of seats. I spy a three-card-draw table and sit down. Faith sits next to me, and we set our chips up in front of us. Expecting to lose everything, I throw my entire stack at the first hand. Fuck it; being reserved is for suckers. Faith sits this one out.

My two cards come. Cowboys, pocket kings. I'm golden. Dealer winds up with A7 off suit. Next card is a five. Big win.

Faith joins in the next hand, and we play up until the last hand, taking the house for everything we can. At the end of the last hand, we're up another three thousand dollars. We tip the dealer, and she thanks us; then, we move to the bar.

Up on the top deck, we watch Canaveral reapproach. A tugboat moves past us, off to guide something larger safely in. We toast to our good luck while a small part of my consciousness watches everyone around us; the last thing I want is to get jacked in the parking lot with all of this cash in our pockets. The Caribbean music plays until we dock. I'm happy to see a few cop cars in the lot as we walk down the gangplank. The old people, vagabonds, and young people all walk back to their cars. Some move quicker than others.

Back over the bridges where Faith closes her eyes and on to the stretch of tinderbox 528. Despite the time of year, the long, flat road is enough to put you back into hibernation. There are cars with plates from every state, busses, and utility vehicles all playing tag just over the speed limit as the dry, unmoving trees race by the windows. It's about as boring as you can get, so we pull out a bottle I keep stashed under the seat and start trading shots. It doesn't take long for our spirits to be high enough with the booze and the winnings to forget the dreary road in front of us.

"Hey, put on that hair metal CD," I suggest to Faith.

She counters with, "How about that dart mix CD I made?" and I know at this point there's no way I'm getting to hear what I want to hear, but with three grand in my pocket, we could listen to polka and I wouldn't give a damn.

We pop in her mix. "Come Undone" by Duran Duran starts off, and so we drive to it. She dances in her seat, fanning herself with hundred-dollar bills. The trees fly by, the Pac-Man lane dividers pass by even quicker, so we make good time.

About twenty minutes and half a bottle into the return trip, I notice that there's another cop car behind us: another state trooper. I'd been speeding for quite a few miles, but I wasn't alone. *Maybe he will pull someone else over instead?* "Bust a Move" by Special Ed comes on, and for a buzzed second, I wonder if I should do just that.

I don't speed off, and the cop doesn't pull anyone else over. He pulls up right behind us. I'm in the left lane; a semi is blocking my move over to the right lane, and I'm not about to speed enough to get a fifteen-over ticket just to let the cop pass, so I hang in the left lane and drive as straight as I can.

"You okay?" asks Faith.

"Yeah, fine. If this pig gets off my ass, or if this asshole semi moves back on my right. Put the bottle back under the seat."

The semi does not move back despite the trooper now flashing his lights and letting his siren go, so I am stuck in the left lane being told to pull over, and I am left with nowhere to pull over to. I'm getting frustrated, but I start to slow down.

I'm looking for a place to pull over, when another semi, an 18-wheeler with trailer, crosses lanes and heads straight for Faith and me. I blink a few times and wonder if the booze was laced with something.

"Um," I say lazily over to Faith, "is that huge-ass truck crossing the highway into our lane?"

Faith doesn't respond. Special Ed continues to "Bust a Move" on the stereo.

Behind the wheel, I have a few seconds to determine what my move will be before we are pulverized by the oncoming several-ton machine. I choose to accelerate. It seems the best move—avoid all collisions and everyone will be okay; then I can get my ticket and maybe go to jail for a DUI. So much for luck; in just a split second in my mind, the three grand in my pocket is flowing right out of the window and into a lawyer's hands.

I speed up and swerve into the right lane, almost clipping the semi that had been blocking us on the right.

I avoid all collisions, but everyone is not okay.

I can see in my side mirror as the semi plows right into the state trooper, who had no room to the left or right. The trooper's car slides under the semi I had nearly clipped, and the two trucks and the squad car crunch and hiss and squeal and tangle into one large, smoky wreck. Another second later, I see fire as cars traveling behind run straight into the mess of metal and rubber blocking the entire westbound highway.

All through this, I do not drop a single mile per hour. Bust a move.

I keep driving at the same speed, still somehow, in some reality, expecting to be pulled over for my minor infraction. But obviously, that's not going to happen now.

Faith, unsure of what to do, yells, "You have to pull over! You have to..." and that is all Faith has to say.

"What would we say? Sorry, officer, I was being chased for speeding, and your buddy got creamed by a semi?"

"But we are witnesses," she says.

"I'm...other than serve as witnesses—of which I am sure there are several—what else can we do? I'm not sure what to do. But I'm not seeing much point in stopping. If we want, we can call in our eyewitness account from home."

Faith thinks for a moment, says, "All right," and then reaches under the seat and pulls the bottle back out. She takes a large swig and then passes it to me. I do the same.

At home, the drinks are made quietly. We wander around, possibly avoiding each other, possibly circling each other, until we both wind up sitting on the couch in front of the television. We're waiting for the news to cover the story. All the while, I feel Faith's spirits diminishing and my hopes of staying out of jail increasing. All of my thoughts feel like flies around me, buzzing and random, and it makes me feel old and exhausted.

"So did they see us?" Faith asks finally.

"I have no idea, babe," I reply, honestly but flatly.

"Is it unlucky to be a part of what happened and not report it, or is it lucky that we got away without a ticket and drunk-driving arrest?" she asks. I understand her dilemma, and it is not harmless or cute. It is genuine and valid; she really is looking for the answer this time.

I think of things to say, but I also do not know the real answer. Perhaps it is a little bit of both, but that solves nothing. It doesn't tell Faith where her luck lies here and now. It lies *there*—someplace without description, but a place that exists.

I answer her as best I can, "I have no idea, babe."

We sit there for two hours and just drink. We don't make any calls; we just wait for the news to put something up about the incident. Finally, the ten o'clock news comes on; there's no mention of the accident at all. I wonder, *Is it because it is a tourist alley?*

But my wonderings are brought short soon enough. Faith has laid out a board game on the coffee table.

"To take our minds off this...this," she says, trailing off while fervently setting up pieces on a board.

I sit there for a moment and then ask her to hand me the playing piece for the corner of my part of the board. She hands me a small, silver race car, and we are all set for a game.

And on the television, a commercial plays. We both watch the commercial, knowing that as soon as it is finished, the news will continue on.

CPSIA information can be obtained at www.ICGtesting.com
Printed in the USA
LVOW122018080512
280882LV00001B/84/P